EMPTY Promises

a novella

ELLE BROOKS

Copyright © 2015 Elle Brooks
This work is registered with and protected by Copyright House & UKCS.

First Edition: March 2015
Library of Congress Cataloging-in-Publication Data
  Brooks, Elle
    Empty Promises / Elle Brooks – 1st ed
      ISBN-13: 978-0-9929888-5-2

  1.   Empty Promises—Fiction 2. Fiction—Novella

http://ellebrooksauthor.com

Emily

What would you do if you knew
when you were going to die?

Would you will death to come and claim you quickly?
Or would you pray for more time?

It wasn't until I knew that I was about to die,
that I decided to really live.

And it wasn't until I gave up on love,
that I finally found it.

Just not in any of the places that I'd been searching.

Sometimes you don't get the fairytale happily ever after,
but if you're lucky, you get so much more.

You get a perfect beginning that you can keep hold
of until the end

Note to the Reader

For fans of *Promises Hurt* and *Forgotten Promises*,
who wanted to know more of Emily's story,
a novella prequel.
For those of you yet to read the Promises series,
this novella can be read as a standalone.

"Somebody should tell us,
right at the start of our lives,
that we are dying.
Then we might live life to the limit,
every minute of every day.
Do it! I say.
Whatever you want to do, do it now!
There are only so many tomorrows."

-Pope Paul VI

Prologue

Emily

I ONCE SAW a postcard in the mall that read: "We do not remember days. We remember moments." It had a picture of two little girls walking away from the camera, holding hands. I bought it because it reminded me of my best friend, Blair. I'm looking at it now. The corners are curled at the edges and the sun, which shines directly on my notice board through my bedroom window, has bleached the picture. It looks almost vintage. I like it better this way.

I remember tacking it to the board and thinking that the postcard was true. Most of my memories are of specific moments in time, and although I can recall the events with virtually perfect clarity, I can't place the dates. There are two exceptions though; two instances that have occurred, and I will forever remember those days. The moment I was diagnosed with Leukemia on August 16th, 2011, and the moment I was told it was terminal on June 2nd, 2013.

The postcard was wrong.

It lied to me, just like everyone in my life has since my first diagnosis.

My naïve, fifteen-year-old self believed the soothing words of encouragement. "You're strong," my parents said.

"You're responding well to the chemotherapy," the doctors told me. "Everything will work out just fine," Blair promised.

My hardened, cynical eighteen-year-old self now knows better.

Wishing for something with all of your heart doesn't make it happen. Not everyone is afforded a happily ever after. If my life were to be documented, it wouldn't be the fairytale that we all dream our lives will be. No, mine would be a Shakespearian tragedy. I'm the protagonist who's cloaked in doom and will ultimately die young, only having experienced unrequited love, empty promises and sadly, not a whole lot more.

Chapter 1

I'M MAD.

No, scratch that.

I'm so far beyond mad that I can't even see straight.

Dr. Zahn said that there are typically five stages of acceptance: denial, anger, bargaining, grieving … and finally, if you're lucky, the acceptance phase. I spent all of last week, after the death sentence the hospital issued me, in stage one. I refused to accept their prognosis and begged for them to run more blood work. Facts are facts, though, and when your bone marrow is spitting out leukemic cells like water from a fire hose, there's little anyone can do to stop the impending flood.

I did the whole clichéd, *Oh, my god, this can't be happening to me* breakdown right then and there in my oncology consultant's office. Blair, Mom, and Dad sat silently; I think they were in shock. Interestingly enough, not one of us cried. They sat like rabbits in headlights, while I paced the room, refusing to accept the words being spoken. We left the hospital with vacant looks plastered over our faces, the news still floating around in our heads, refusing to seep in.

I woke up this morning feeling … different than the previous few days. I think I've graduated from denial and have boarded a raft, ready to navigate the treacherous waters of anger. It's as if someone's unleashed the freaking Kraken.

Mom is the first to feel my wrath.

She brings me a glass of orange juice to take with my Dexamethasone because she forgot the hospital withdrew my treatment schedule and replaced it with a palliative care plan. I scream at her—a blood-curdling high-pitched wail of a scream. She cries, then I cry and apologize before retreating back to my bedroom.

I catch my reflection as I cross the room and notice the breakout over my forehead and cheeks; it's just another thing to add to the "Stuff That Sucks in the Life of Emily Wilson" list. Taking me off of my daily dose of chemo has my body in shock, and the toxins need an outlet, so my face seems to be it. When my treatment was stopped for a couple of weeks after I contracted e-coli last summer, the spots came and went pretty quickly, but a deep purple rash over your face is embarrassing and hard to hide.

I suppose I should focus on the good points:

1. I'm not feeling sick.

I've been on medication for so long that my body's used to the feeling of being continuously not quite one hundred percent. It's like my *normal* has been reset now that the drugs have stopped and are leaving my system.

2. I have energy instead of feeling bone tired.

I wasn't even aware my energy levels had changed. *Weird, huh?* I don't want to get too excited; soon the cancer will kick my ass, and I won't have chemo as a buffer so the meds will start again. I should treat this stage as a gift because I'm not sure how long I'll feel this good. *Good...*

What a cruel joke this is becoming.

ele

It's been almost three hours of rocking back and forth on the bed, trying to calm the urge to smash and destroy anything and everything.

I'm a mess.

I'm a horrible daughter.

I'm dying.

I hear the doorbell chime and then the sound of the door being opened. I don't need to go and see who it is; I know it's Blair. She always lets herself in but makes sure to ring the bell first. It started when we were around thirteen years old. Our paths must have crossed as I'd made my way to her house at the same time that she'd decided to come over here. My parents, much to my complete horror, had taken the opportunity for a nooner. Blair walked in on them in the kitchen as my dad was buttoning up his pants and my mom was flustered and fixing her shirt. She's always used the doorbell without fail ever since. I'd have found the whole situation much more amusing, had it not been my parents. Ew!

I hear her shout her hellos to my parents, then I wait

the few seconds it takes for her to reach my room and crack the door.

"You awake?" she asks quietly as she peeks her head in. She enters when she notices me sitting amidst the rumpled sheets of my bed.

"I'll warn you now," I tell her sternly, "I'm in a shitty mood and I don't have the energy to smile and fake it 'til I make it."

"That's okay. I've come to wallow with you. School was a nightmare yesterday. I don't think I can face going back Monday morning. I swear that you not being there tilts my axis. Want to hear something that will no doubt make you smile?" she asks, widening her eyes. It sounds like she's issuing a dare.

"Go on, then." I raise what's left of my thinning brow. *You're gonna fail* I think as I issue a bored stare. She smirks, and I mirror it.

"Okay, you ready for this?" She wiggles around on the bed, getting comfy. "My mom made breakfast burritos for me yesterday to try and cheer me up." She lets out a little grimace as if she's feeling bad for mentioning that she's been upset. "Anyway, you know me and Mexican food … I ate three and then headed off to school, just like I would any other day. I make my way to first period AP English and my tummy starts to churn. I'm thinking it's probably because I stuffed myself with enough food to feed a small army and then rushed to get to class on time, so I ignored it. But the churning didn't subside—it got worse."

"Um, okay then. So you had a stomach ache at school … what's funny about that?"

4

She shakes her head a little and a flash of humiliation passes across her face. Her thick chocolate hair is piled messily on top of her head and her glasses slip as she scrunches her nose. "I haven't finished yet. So yeah, my stomach was beginning to cramp and I didn't feel at all well, so I raised my hand and asked to be excused. Mr. Wilde gave this stupid speech about using the restrooms before class like we were all a bunch of kindergarteners, which was only mildly embarrassing in the scheme of things. By that time, he'd shifted the entire class's focus on to me and I was getting really desperate. He told me I could be excused and I practically jumped from my seat, ready to haul ass to the bathroom. The movement didn't agree with me though. I let out the biggest fart you have ever heard. It was awful. Everyone, and I do mean EVE-REEEY-ONE, burst out laughing. Even Mr. Wilde.

"That's not even the worse part. It smelled so freaking bad that Jen Gray and Ali Greig, who were in the row behind me, actually started to gag. And not the dramatic fake kind either. It was real. Don't even get me started on the crazy Asian girl that they hang with. You know, the one TJ Connors so affectionately labeled the 'Crazian'. Nobody has been able to understand a thing that's come out of her mouth all semester since she transferred. Seems that the language barrier has been removed now, which meant that the whole class could hear and understand when she managed to shout, 'Oh, my eyes are burning!' in perfect freaking English! Damn Mexican food!"

I don't want to laugh.

I want to reel in my anger and self-pity.

But how can I not?

I feel my cheeks begin to rise and a smile tug at the corner of my lips before I give in and fall backward on my bed giggling. "Oh my god, I wish I'd seen that!"

"Trust me, you did not want to see it—or smell it, for that matter. Seriously, why does this shit always happen to me? I should be banned from public spaces." She grins, falling down beside me. She knows, easy as that, her work here is complete. She's successfully pulled me out of my stupor in two minutes flat.

For now...

elle

"So I'll wait out here for you, and then we're going for ice-cream if you feel up to it." Blair motions to the white leather couches of Dr. Zahn's waiting room. It feels more like a glossy, high-end reception of a media company with all the chrome, glass and white Barcelona chairs. I take a deep breath, and the smell of the calla lilies sitting in a huge glass vase on the sectional table infiltrates my senses. I should probably dislike it here, but I don't. I *almost* enjoy talking to Dr. Zahn; she doesn't look at me with pity in her eyes. I respect that.

"Okay, thirty minutes. Yeah." I look at the only other person in the waiting room. He's a tall blond guy with messy hair and an obnoxiously tight gray T-shirt that reads, "This is my happy face!" in bold, black letters. I nod my head in his direction, grinning at Blair. They'd make a great match; she loves her slogan tees. "Have fun," I murmur, trying to alert her to the guy's presence, but she's oblivious.

6

"Good afternoon, Emily. Is your mother not joining us today?" the doctor asks as she moves from behind her desk over to the chairs positioned around a small, circular, glass table in the corner of her office.

"Not today. Blair brought me. She's in the waiting room," I answer as I take a seat.

"Very well. Let's get started and not keep her waiting." I watch as she shrugs out of her pale-blue suit jacket and drapes it over the back of her chair. "How are you feeling today?"

It's such a simple question; one that most people could probably answer subconsciously. Not me, though. A million emotions stir in my stomach and chest, and my mind grasps at the first thought that enters it.

"Cheated."

ele

"She wants you to keep a diary?" Blair asks as we're walking through the mall, our trajectory set to Joe's Creamery.

"Yeah, you know what shrinks are like—they love for you to document your feelings. I don't know … I mean, it's not like I don't sort of do it anyway. You know I write in my journal most days."

"So what are you going to do? Just carry on with that or start a new one?" she asks as we reach the parlor's entrance.

A bunch of hyped-up kids barrel through the door holding half-eaten cones dripping with chocolate and sprinkles, knocking us out of their way. A frazzled-looking woman, I'm guessing their mom, rushes after them. She shoots us an apologetic look as she simultaneously shouts at the kids not to run or touch anything with sticky fingers, all the while balancing her purse and a heap of jackets and toys under her arms. I watch as the woman struggles.

I'm jealous.

Jealous of troubles I'm never going to have. The feeling burns in my chest as though I've just chugged a scalding hot cup of coffee, setting fire to my insides. "I'm not sure yet … probably a new one. Anyway, let's not talk about cancer diaries. I need ice-cream!".

Chapter 2

July 16th, 2013
(*5 months)

Dear Diary,

So I've decided to take Dr. Zahn's advice and keep a diary about how I'm feeling. Although, I'm doing things a little differently than what she suggested. Instead of it being all about this stupid, cruel disease—which, by the way, fuck you, cancer—I've decided to write it as a memoir. At least this way I'm leaving something behind; I'm leaving my mark. It's not exactly going to be a huge mark. In fact, it will probably be more of a scuff, but it's something.

I have no idea how to write a memoir, so bear with me.

I'm still mad. It's been two weeks since the news of my impending doom, and I'm still floating in the anger stages of my five-step grief process. I'm hoping it will pass soon; I'm looking forward to stage five—acceptance. I can't see me reaching it any time soon, which makes me sad, especially since time is now working against me. My parents are putting on a brave face; I know it's for my sake, but I kind of just want them to act normal around me. I can tell they're holding back, scared that they'll upset me if they cry in my presence, but it makes me feel guilty. They should be allowed to grieve. I wouldn't mind.

Anyway, on that happy note! Blair has been amazing; she's been here every day, updating me on the lunchroom gossip. Apparently, Jen Gray is sleeping with Coach Carter. I'd have said no way, but thinking about it, Jen would sleep with anything with a pulse. Coach Carter's kept her behind a few times in gym class to help put away equipment. She's not exactly built for lugging around apparatuses so I actually think this particular nugget of information could be true.

Blair also mentioned that Kickstart is playing a gig at some bar in town next week. I think we should go; I'm missing my daily dose of Ethan Jamison. It's kind of crazy to miss something you never had, but I do. We've barely spoken, yet I miss him like we've been a couple for years and have been cruelly separated. I'm one of around a thousand of his friends on Facebook, so I click on his profile daily in hopes that he's posted something that will give me my daily fix. He never does.

That's kind of creepy, isn't it? I should maybe tear out this entry and re-write it without sounding like a psycho stalker. Even if the term does kind of fit.

Blair often tries to make me feel better by referring to it as taking a 'covert active interest.' Mom keeps it real; she tells us that no matter how we dress it up, we're no better than a pair of peeping Toms. Apparently, taking selfies with him in the background is a breach of his privacy. Of course, that doesn't stop her from looking at the snaps. I'm pretty sure she finds him almost as hot as I do. We saw him a few months back coming out of a pizza place and she elbowed me, pointing him out and muttering under her breath something about being twenty years younger. Dad laughed until he caught sight of Ethan for himself. Then he went off about how he was just as well built and good looking in high school. He'd scoffed that he'd better have some sort of talent or work ethic because his looks will soon fade. Mom and I burst out laughing; it was equal parts amusing and gross that my dad was entering into some weird pissing contest with Ethan Jamison, without the poor guy even knowing about it.

When we returned home that evening, Dad spent a half hour in the basement searching through boxes until he returned wearing a slightly beat-up leather, biker-style jacket. It wasn't too dissimilar to the one Ethan was wearing. Mom's face lit up, and then—in a weird, husky voice—she made some suggestion about leaving the jacket out for later. I'm sure I threw up a little in my mouth. Mom and Dad were high-school sweethearts; they've been together since they were juniors and they were each other's first real relationship. Mom once told me that they were each other's one and only in the sexual sense. It's not something a fourteen-year-old wants to hear, especially in front of her best friend, but she was determined to give me the 'sex' talk. I told her that it was unnecessary and then she almost had a heart attack, thinking I meant that I was already sexually active. It took Blair and me almost an hour to convince her that I meant I learned the birds and bees stuff way before her little sex talk ambush. When we finally escaped my mom and headed over to Blair's house, Susan couldn't stop laughing at how mortified we both were. Little did we realize she was lulling us into a false sense of security. We were bombarded with handfuls of pamphlets on birth control and teenage pregnancy statistics. Sometimes I think parents are put on this earth solely to embarrass us.

I had always envisioned my first time would be with Ethan Jamison; we'd fall madly in love and get married and produce a whole orchestra full of beautifully musical little mini-mes. Our children would have my hair (pre-chemo) and his eyes, and they'd all play instruments and we'd be like an updated version of the von Trapp family, minus that Nazi regime and shit.

Guess it will always be a dream now.

Considering that I have roughly six months to make it all happen, I should probably just focus on the "getting him to even notice me" part. Okay, that settles it, I'm going to his gig, I'm going to talk to him, and I'm going to make my play. I refuse to leave this life without at least experiencing kissing the man of my dreams just once. After all, what do I have to lose?

Watch. This. Space!

Chapter 3

July 17th, 2013

Dear Diary,

Operation "MRS. JAMISON" has commenced. Okay, so I know the title needs work, but Emily Jamison has a certain ring to it. Blair's on board with going to the Kickstart gig and has even agreed to come shopping with me later today. If I'm about to make a play for the hottest guy at school, I need to do it looking my best and I've lost so much weight lately that I need something new that actually fits. I've always maintained that if you feel good, you look good.

On a plus note, this little mission is giving me something to actually look forward to.

July 17th, 2013

I couldn't wait until tomorrow to update this because I might forget something!

I have just experienced probably the funniest shopping trip I will ever have. My poor best friend!

Blair collected me at lunch and we headed to the mall; I saw a pair of killer jeans and decided to try them on. I've always been a confident person and I like to think I have a good eye for what suits me, but my body shape has changed so much since starting treatment that I wanted a second opinion. I called Blair into the changing room and made some asinine comment about my steroids making me look like I have the body of a twelve-year-old boy. I hadn't needed her opinion really because anyone could see that the jeans looked horrendous, but I'd wanted to vent.

She'd laughed and scrunched her nose, telling me, "Yep, those are definitely not the right cut for you anymore. Shame though—they're cute."

"You should take them and try them on. They'd look good on you," I'd said, slipping the jeans down my legs and shoving them into her arms.

She unbuckled her belt and wiggled out of her shorts before shaking out the jeans in front of me. By this time, I'd changed back into my own clothes and was waiting on her. She pulled the jeans up over her knees and then did a little jump to hoist them up further. We used to be the same size, but apparently, we're not anymore. She held onto the belt loops as she shimmied them up but somehow lost her balance. I think I was in some sort of suspended animation as everything unfolded.

Blair stumbled into the side of the cubicle, and the rail that held the curtain slipped from its mount and came crashing down. At the same time, one side of the cubicle collapsed and crashed into the next. We both watched in horror at the domino effect; one by one the five cubicles in the women's changing room came crashing down around us. It sounded like an earthquake. I took one look at her panic-stricken face and did what any best friend would do…

I burst out laughing.

The sales assistants came running through to see what had happened. Not just the female ones, either; the two hot guys who worked the men's section came flying in, sneakers screeching as they skidded to an abrupt stop. By this time, I was sitting amongst the curtains on the store floor in fits of laughter, tears streaming down my face as she stood like a deer in the headlights. The jeans were still halfway up her thighs and she was wearing a bright blue thong that had the word 'ANGRY' above a picture of a cartoon beaver. That wasn't even the best part, though; her ass was projected onto all the mirrors throughout the room and no matter what angle she tried to turn, the image was still reflected.

I'm never going to win bestie of the year, but I can't remember the last time I laughed so hard. I really need to buy her a present for being such a douche. We left after that; guess I'll have to get Mom to take me shopping later in the week.

I quickly close the screen on my Mac, hiding my diary entries as my door opens and Mom's head peeps through. I haven't told her what I'm doing. I'm not sure I'm ready for her to know just yet.

"Hey, sweetheart, you have visitors."

"Okay, be right out."

I'm not expecting anyone, and Blair's already left for the day, so I'm not sure who would be dropping in on me unannounced. I pull my shirt tighter around me—I can't seem to stay warm lately—and make my way through to the kitchen.

I can hear Casey's unmistakable drawl as she chats animatedly to my dad. Brie jumps off the barstool to greet me with a hug; her white and blue cheer uniform flashes before my eyes as she moves at warp speed and squeezes me tight.

"Em, girl, we've missed you!" Casey shouts as she makes her way over.

Dad looks relieved that her attention's been stolen and slips out of the room, widening his eyes at me as he slinks through the door as if to wish me luck.

The girls are great; we've been on the cheer squad together all through school and the two of them come as a package; you don't see one without the other. I guess you could say the same about Blair and me, except Casey and Brie are always off-the-chart hyper. We're all close friends, although I think they intimidate Blair a little. The two of them together are a lot to handle for *anyone*.

"We came to see if you wanted to hang out," Brie says, taking a step back out of my personal space so I can actually breathe.

"If you're feeling up to it, that is. We're going to catch a movie, but we don't have to if you don't feel like it," Casey interrupts. She regards me like I'm some fragile china doll she's worried to play with for fear it might break.

"Count me in. Do I have time to change?"

16

"Yay! Told you she'd say yes!" Brie shouts at Case. Her blond hair and boobs bounce all over the place as she hops with excitement; anyone would think she'd just won the lotto.

"Yeah, yeah, I think you need to lay off the caffeine. You're making me feel dizzy bouncing around. I'm cutting you off."

"She bet me $10 you'd flake on us," Brie offers as Casey's face contorts in horror.

"That sounds way worse than it was," she says, shooting Brie a death glare. "Blair mentioned you guys were at the mall today, I just said to *Skippy* here that you'd probably be too tired to hang out."

"Relax, you don't need to explain," I tell her, walking back to my room to grab a sweater.

ele

"So, what do you guys want to see?"

"I'm easy," Brie says, rocking back and forth on her heels.

The sound of us shouting, "We know!" in unison makes her visibly startle. She rolls her eyes at us in feigned indignation before turning towards the popcorn stand.

"Oh my god. Don't look now, but guess who's here?" she whisper shouts. Casey and I turn to see who she's talking about. "I said, don't look now!" she grits out.

"Seriously, saying that is like offering cake to a fat kid. Of course we're going to look," Casey sniggers as I stand rooted to the spot, staring unashamedly at Ethan

17

Jamison as he talks to Jackson and TJ, two of the members of his band.

"Good god those boys are hot," Case says as she nudges my arm.

"What? Yeah … hot," I practically dribble out as I continue with my moronic staring. I can hear Casey laugh at me, and then Brie says something back to her before heading off in the guy's direction.

"Wait, where the hell's she going?" I hiss as I watch her approach Ethan and his friends.

"To see if they wanna join us."

"What! No … she can't. I mean, they can't … I mean … shit."

"Wow, you really do lose the ability to form a coherent sentence when Ethan Jamison is in the vicinity, don't you?"

"Ugh … Seriously, how can she just walk over there and strike up a conversation? I know she's not immune to that particular group of guy's looks. Hell, I'm fifty feet away and they've reduced me to pathetic little girl status without even knowing I'm here. I'd give anything to just be able to go up and talk to him."

"Him?" Casey asks, raising her perfectly arched eyebrow at me.

I feel my cheeks redden. "I meant them."

"Course you did, sweetie."

"Oh, shut up." I smile until I notice Brie heading back to us with Ethan, Jackson and TJ in tow.

"Better close your mouth, Emily, you're drooling," Casey murmurs before stepping forward to say hello.

I'm so not prepared for this. I look down at my ballet

pumps, faded skinny jeans and rumpled cream sweater. This is not how I wanted to look when I finally spoke to him. *Damn it, damn it, damn it.*

Lord, just take me now.

"Hey," Jackson greets, and the other two nod their heads, acknowledging my presence without actually having to converse. They all know Brie and Casey, but to be fair, I don't think there's a single guy in the whole of our senior class who doesn't at least know of them. They're equal parts stunning, popular and nice; not traits that usually go together with pretty girls. Della and Dannii, another two girls from our squad, unashamedly demonstrate that. They're our school's version of the typical clichéd mean girls. It's kind of a shame; up until last year, Dannii seemed to be a genuinely nice girl, but then she started to hang out with Della more. The transformation was pretty rapid. It was like zero to bitch in one week flat.

From the corner of my eye, I can see TJ studying me as Ethan and Jackson talk with the girls. I'm instantly self-conscious. I used to have a thing where I twiddled with my hair when I was anxious, and I'd be doing it right now if I had enough to twist. My pixie-length blond hair is barely long enough to run my fingers through. I smile at him because really, what else can I do? He grins back, although I can tell he's deliberating about whether or not to talk to me. His smile, although polite, doesn't reach his eyes, and the way his hands are stuffed deep into his pockets makes him look uncomfortable. He's rocking back and forth on his heels and I'm sure he's waiting for someone to jump in, call for his attention and rescue him.

I like to consider myself a pretty approachable person, but since being diagnosed, people seem to have forgotten how to talk to me like a regular girl. It was all good until I lost my hair. Blair and I buzzed our heads before mine could all fall out, and instantly, people's reactions towards me changed. The bald head is a beacon for "this girl must be sick."

I remember the first day I walked into the teenage oncology unit. The dayroom was like a sea of pale-faced teens, each battling with varying amounts of hair loss. It shocked me almost as much as the initial diagnosis, but what eventually became normal for me still took other people by surprise.

"You're Emily, right?"

I'm about to answer, but he tags on, "the girl with cancer," to the end of his question and I almost choke on my tongue. I should be used to people without filters, but it still gets me that they seem to think cancer is my defining feature.

"That's me," I say, pulling out my cell to give myself a distraction.

"So, how's that going? You on treatment still? Or are you, you know, okay now?"

Well, fuck, this is awkward. I look up from my cell to see him push his hands even deeper into his pockets. He looks really uncomfortable at having to make conversation with me. The rest of the guys are still talking animatedly amongst themselves.

"I'm okay," I lie. I tell myself that it's to spare him the mortification and discomfort that would no doubt ensue after asking the terminally ill chick if she's cured, but if I'm honest with myself, it's to save my own embarrassment.

"Awesome," he replies, looking genuinely happy for me.

I almost groan as I attempt to smile, but it's so strained I'm sure it looks more menacing than anything else. An obstinate silence descends for what feels like a ridiculously long amount of time before Brie finally turns and links her arm through mine.

"Okay, the boys are getting the tickets, and we need to go get the snacks." I let her lead me away as I mentally prepare myself for the next few hours.

Casey and Brie are paying as I struggle with pulling my sweater off; my little exchange with TJ left me hot and bothered, and not in a good way. I drape the top over my arm and look up to see Ethan standing in front of me, merely inches away.

"Cool shirt," he says with a crooked grin as he thrusts his hand out towards me. I look down to see I'm wearing one of Dad's old Pink Floyd tees that my Mom shrunk years ago; I'd immediately claimed it. It's one of my favorites.

"Thanks," I reply a little more zealously than intended. He's still holding his arm out towards me and I scrunch my nose in confusion.

"Your ticket."

"Huh? Oh, my ticket, right. Thanks."

He hands it over and waits a beat before asking if I'm all right. *Great, I'm obviously making a stellar impression.* I nod, and he turns to join the rest of his friends. Just like that, I nose dive straight off his radar.

Excellent.

Chapter 4

"ARE YOU GOING to eat that?"

I look down at the salad I'm pushing around on my plate and then back up to meet Blair's worried stare.

"I've got no appetite," I tell her, shoving my plate to the side. My agitation is almost palpable. I watch as she lets her fork drop with an obnoxiously loud clatter and then sits back in her seat, folding her arms.

"You need to cheer up. It was just one night at the movies, and you'll likely have another opportunity to speak to him. We're still going to the Kickstart gig next week, so you could talk to him there," she says, willing me to stop with the moping.

"I know. I'm just a little gutted that the only interaction I've had with him resulted in me standing and looking completely vacant and spaced out. You only get one chance at a first impression, and mine sucked."

"Well, if you really did 'drop off his radar,'" she says, doing finger quotes, "he won't remember meeting you."

"Jeez, thanks. Way to make a girl feel good about herself!"

"Oh, calm it. I just mean that if he doesn't remember you, you get a second chance at your first impression. Silver linings and all that!"

"And if he does remember me?" I grimace.

"Well, then you're already winning. He'll know who you are, which means he took an interest the first time you spoke, and you just need to unleash the funny, witty, slightly mental Emily I know and love. You'll dazzle him, and if he's not ass-over-tit madly in love with you inside of thirty seconds, the guy's a moron. And honestly, Em, who wants to date a moron?"

"Me!"

She leans forward to push my shoulder as she laughs and orders, "Come on, let's head to class," clearing our table and placing the tray on the racks as we make our way out of the cafeteria. We normally sit in the quad, but I'm cold as hell today, even though everyone else is walking around in T-shirts.

I decided that I needed some normality back in my life, so Mom called the school and arranged for me to return. There's only a finite amount of trash daytime television you can watch before your brain turns to mush; the prospect of becoming a *Real Housewives* addict became scarily appealing and an actual probability.

The news of my terminal status seems to have already made the rounds, which is kind of a relief. I didn't want to come back to questions about my treatment, so I'd asked Brie to inform the cheer team of my plight. Blair had said that the quickest way to pass the news through the school was to confide in the cheerleaders. She was adamant that if they thought it was a secret, the whole town would know inside of forty-eight hours. Turns out, she was right. It's an oddly impressive and efficient gossip grapevine they operate.

I spent most of yesterday trying to ward off looks of sympathy; I was worried that I would arrive at school today and be faced with more of the same. I needn't have worried, though—this is high school, after all. My news has already been bumped from the top spot amidst the hype of an apparent R-rated tape of Jennifer Gray and some unidentified old dude doing the rounds on Facebook. It seems to be the only thing anyone is discussing today. I hope I see her; I could kiss her for taking the heat off me.

We finally round the corner to AP English and are met by a set of abs, seemingly made of steel. My reactions aren't quick enough to avoid the collision into Jackson's broad chest and I face plant into his pectorals before stumbling backward. He lunges forward to pull me upright just as Blair lurches me into her side to try and steady me. I feel like a rag doll.

"Sorry! Emily, isn't it?" he asks. "I didn't see you there. I haven't hurt you, have I?" I can tell from his panic-stricken face and his slight overreaction to our minor collision that he knows I'm sick.

"Yeah, no worries," I reassure him. He actually looks pale. The poor guy probably thinks I'm about to keel over and die.

"Okay, well, sorry again," he says with a rueful smile, sidestepping past me and disappearing around the corner.

Jackson comes across quite sweet. He's tall, blond, built and gorgeous. And he has the reputation to go with his looks. He's a certified man-whore, just like his best friend and my infatuation. You would think knowing this about Ethan would lessen my affections towards him, but it doesn't deter me; not even a little. I'm certain there's something more to him than what he projects, and I would give just about anything to be the one to discover what that is.

"Earth to Em … you sure you're okay?" Blair asks, scanning me like she's looking for broken bones.

"I'm all right. Seriously though, his chest—it didn't give even a little. It was like a slab of marble. Is it wrong that I want to see it bare now?"

"Oh my gosh, you're incorrigible! But no, I'd sign up for that particular peep show too. Shame he's such a slut. He's cute."

"Hold the phone. Blair Thomas is actually declaring a guy cute!" I say, mocking the fact that Blair almost never shows an interest in guys.

"I'm not blind, Emily. I just have a good check on my hormonal state, unlike you." She sticks her tongue out at me as we head into the classroom.

I don't attempt a retort because I know as well as she so obviously does that when it comes to Ethan and the rest of Kickstart, I'm about as chemically balanced as a frat boy at his first mixer.

July 23rd, 2013
Dear Diary,

Dr. Zahn seems happy with my decision to go back to school. She was also impressed that I've taken her up on this cancer diary malarkey. Truth is, I think it's helping to write this stuff down. I'm not angry anymore, which is a good thing, but I'm not sure where I am on my little route to acceptance. Supposedly, I should be in the bargaining phase, but I'm not. I gave up on the bargaining idea, and pleading with God that I'd be a better person and go to church every Sunday without fail; that I'd start doing more things for charity, and even abstain from alcohol, drugs and sex before marriage. Not that honoring that part would be hard.

I was a model teenager, and the cancer still came back.

I haven't lost my faith in God, per se. I need to believe that there's something more for me after this. There just has to be because the alternative is too scary to wrap my mind around.

I caught my dad praying last night; he's not religious, not even a little. I'd gone to get a glass of water in the middle of the night and he was sitting at the kitchen island. His hands were clasped in prayer while muttering something under his breath with a glass of whiskey sitting by his side. His eyes were red and glassy when he looked up and noticed me.

My dad is a good-looking guy. All my friends have crushed on him at one point or another … well, all except Blair, that is. He's tall, broad and has an athletic physique. Unlike most of the school dads, he still has a head full of thick blond hair—there's not a solitary grey in sight—and he always looks put together.

Until that moment.

He was slouched into the chair with his shoulders

rounded, looking half his normal size. I felt my stomach squeeze as I took in the grey pallor of his skin and his disheveled hair, which like he'd spent all day and night clutching at it. I stood still in the doorway, not knowing whether to go to him or give him his moment. I've only seen my dad cry maybe three times my whole life.

He made the decision for me, ushering me inside and making me a cup of hot milk. He hasn't done that since I was at least seven. I reveled in his tenderness as he pulled me down onto his lap and cuddled me until I'd finished it. We didn't speak, not a single word. It felt like it used to do when I'd have a bad dream and he'd stay with me snuggled into his chest until I felt safe enough to fall back to sleep. It was comforting until I noticed his breathing stutter, like he was trying to swallow a sob. Then it felt like a goodbye.

I'm not sure how long we were in the kitchen, but I remember waking as he carried me back to my room and tucked me safely into my bed.

I don't know why I'm documenting this, but I just can't stop thinking about it. Dad, if you ever find yourself reading this—I love you. All the years I've spent with you and Mom are worth all the years that I'll have to spend without you. Like you've always said: If you count all the waves in all the oceans, that's how much I love you.

Chapter 5

I MADE A list—a bucket list, I guess you could call it.

I decided shorty after my first diagnosis that there were certain things that I wanted to achieve. Not grand or necessarily even important accomplishments that would garner any accolades, but things that were significant to me. I didn't devise it with the morbid thought that I was going to die; it was more of a reminder to actually live my life and make use of my time.

If there is such a thing as a positive side to Leukemia, it's that it makes you slow down and evaluate your existence. You begin to notice the little things and stop taking everything for granted. Take the smell of fresh air: I know it sounds dumb, but after my first six-week stint in the hospital at the beginning of my treatment, I couldn't even leave the unit. I was weak; the asparaginase shots had rendered me fit for a wheelchair, and the rest of the chemo cocktail had my mouth so sore that it hurt to talk. I was at a whole new level of depressed that I didn't even know existed. The day I was told I could go home, I almost didn't want to. *What was the point?*

Blair and my mom wheeled me outside as Dad pulled the car around. When we passed the double doors of the hospital entrance, a breeze caught me and I swear the world had never smelled so good. I'd forgotten what the outdoors smelled like, and it was at that moment, as the wind skimmed across my bald head, making me shiver, that I realized how much I loved life.

So yeah, I made a list.

I'm searching my Mac for it now so I can add it into my diary. I click onto the little manila file icon marked 'misc' and up it pops, mocking me with all the empty checkboxes. I've been slowly working to fulfill each point without anyone knowing of its existence. Keeping something like this under wraps is actually a whole lot harder than you would think. I've had to censor myself at times, to make sure I didn't spill and tell anyone. Keeping it from Blair has been the hardest. At first, its anonymity was because it made me somewhat embarrassed. I try and steer clear of anything too cliché, and the cancer patient and her bucket list are the epitome of cliché, but whatever. It has slowly transformed; I'm no longer embarrassed by my pursuit to place a check in each of the checkboxes. It's evolved, and I'm not sure when it happened, but now it's more of a challenge—not physically, but mentally. I wanted something that was just for me; my own achievement, I guess.

I started to feel weighed down with this overwhelming urge to complete the tasks on my own. I don't mean with solitude; in fact, I didn't want help making them happen. I'm sure there would be no shortage of *wish factories* willing to grant me a few, but the rush of making something happen myself is a heady one, and I like the feeling. I suppose that sounds horribly selfish. I'd never really noticed until now.

I press the cursor and read each point, letting the taste of the words linger on my tongue before speaking them aloud. Why does it feel like I'm announcing all my secrets?

I copy and paste the list into today's diary entry.

ele

July 28th, 2013

Dear Diary…

The List

1. ~~Swim with dolphins~~
2. Visit the Grand Canyon
3. Go to Vegas, baby!
4. Sing/Perform for a crowd
5. ~~Tell Mr. Parker he's a dick!~~
6. Skinny dip
7. Get completely wasted
8. ~~Smoke a cigarette~~
9. Fall in love
10. Lose my V card (Ideally Ethan Jamison!)
11. Sleep under the stars
12. ~~Ride a horse~~
13. ~~Volunteer (hospital/old folks' home/ homeless shelter)~~
14. ~~TP Harriet Clare's house~~

15. Ride in a hot air balloon
16. Visit Paris
17. Get a tattoo
18. Send a message in a bottle
19. Dye my hair bright pink
20. Try Surfing

When I wrote this list a couple of years back, I didn't contemplate that it would actually have an expiration date. I'm a positive person, and I saw no reason to believe that I wouldn't beat this disease and live to be a hundred years old. But life, fate, destiny or however you want to term it, had other plans.

I'm sitting here now, staring at quite a few empty boxes on a not very long list and wondering how in the hell I'm going to get it all finished. It has taken the best part of two years to get through half of it, and now I have somewhere around six months to complete the rest. Maybe I need to admit defeat and enlist some help.

Maybe it's time to call Blair.

elle

I do call Blair, but in the time it takes her to answer the phone, I've talked myself out of fessing up about the list. It can wait. Actually, in the cold reality of day, it probably can't, but to hell with it. I owe it to myself to give it one last push. Instead, I tell her about the shopping trip with my mom over the weekend, and how I'd seen at the mall the most beautiful dress ever created. It's a midnight blue, strapless fitted floor-length creation—magnificence born from its simplicity.

I already found a cute, bright-yellow sundress to wear for the Kickstart gig. It was one of Mom's picks. When she handed it to me in the store to try on, I frowned and held it out in front of me in an unimpressed inspection. Don't get me wrong; it looked cute with its thin spaghetti straps and fifties-style cinched waist and flared skirt. But it looked like something you would pair with a cardigan and wear to church on Sundays. I decided that I'd try it on just to appease her hopeful expression. I pulled it over my head in the small cubicle and turned to the mirror to confirm my contempt, but was immediately taken back by my reflection. The color warmed my ever-paling skin tone, and magically gifted me back some of its luminosity. The cut on me was perfect; it created curves where mine once where, and for a second, I felt like the old me. I took in the length of the skirt as it skimmed mid-thigh and smiled. It seemed considerably longer on the hanger. I stared at my reflection, musing at how good the dress was making me feel. I decided that if I teamed it with my black leather jacket and biker boots, it would give it an edge. Plus, together with my cropped hair and some smoky eye makeup, it should hopefully mimic the *Heroine Chic,* European look that British models seem to pull off so effortlessly. Not that I think I look remotely like a model. Or British. I do have the heroine addict look down pat, though.

I grinned at myself as I undressed, thinking about how appearances can be so deceptive. Two minutes earlier I thought this was an outfit for church; now I'm planning to wear it for worshipping someone *entirely* different.

I arranged to meet Blair at her house to get ready for Ethan's show on Friday night. I've already made the conscious decision to cross at least one item off of my list. I figure, where better to get completely trashed for the fist time than at a gig? Alcohol is supposed to lower your inhibitions and give you a heightened state of self-confidence, *right?* If I ply myself with enough of the stuff, I may just have the courage to make my play; plus, the alcohol will surely soften the blow. I know my logic is less than sound, but I'm desperate, and apparently shameless.

Ugh.

ele

Friday rolls around at a glacial pace and I wake in the morning feeling like crap. My newfound get up and go, got up and fucking went. I'm not a huge cusser, but…

FUCK, FUCK, FUCKETY-FUCK!

This is just so typical. I've been so excited about today and now that it's here, all I can concentrate on is the pounding in my head and the invisible weights that have seemingly attached to all of my limbs.

I stalk through the kitchen like a pissed off grizzly bear, fling open the meds cabinet and scramble around for some painkillers. I've not been able to take anything that wasn't prescribed by my oncologist for so long that I pause, momentarily worrying if it will be okay before tossing two pills back and washing them down with a gulp of water directly from the faucet. *What's the worst that could happen? They kill me? Ha! They better get in line.*

I shuffle back to my room and slam the door, wincing as the sound ricochets around my skull as I scowl angrily like it wasn't just me that made it happen. My dress, jacket and boots are displayed in the corner of the room, all ironed and ready to go. I stare at them for a long moment before squaring my shoulders and standing tall. *Fake it 'tll you make it, Wilson.* I strip and head into my bathroom. I'm not going to be beaten, not today.

As I climb into the shower, I decide that I'm gonna suck it up and manipulate this day to go my way, and I'm going to do it with a smile, even if it's forced. Positive Mental Attitude, Emily…

P.M. mother-effing A!

elle

August 2nd, 2013
*(*4 Months)*

Dear Diary,

It's Friday!

I woke up feeling less than stellar, but as the day goes on, I'm feeling better. By the way, I'm using the term 'better' very loosely. I've taken a few pills and they seem to be keeping my headache at bay. Let's hope they can hold out until after the gig.

I'm a ball of nervous energy; if someone came up and touched me right now, I'm sure I'd electrocute them. On one hand, I'm completely amped at the prospect of seeing Ethan, and at the same time, I'm scared to death. I know the chances of tonight playing out anywhere near how I've dreamed are about as likely as my doctor calling and telling me that they messed up the tests and actually, I'm fine. But I can't let go of that little ray of hope—the one tucked down deep at the bottom of my heart—that maybe he'll like me. Not 'friend-zone' like, but 'damn, you're kinda hot' like. I've clearly taken too many meds…

I'll report back after the event.

Wish me luck.

Chapter 6

THE ROOM FEELS heavy with the smell of alcohol and sweat. I'm looking down at the big black stamp on my hand that alerts everyone within a fifty-feet radius that I'm not twenty-one. Last week I'd hit Casey up for her college contact that had supplied some kids with a pretty decent fake ID, but a hundred bucks and a shady looking ID later, I lost my nerve. I didn't hand over the counterfeit license when carded at the club's entrance. So I guess I can forget about crossing 'get wasted' off my list. Maybe it wasn't such a bad thing though; I'm feeling a lot less than okay at the moment. I can feel the makeup I spent a painstakingly long hour applying sliding right off my face with the beads of sweat that have broken out.

"You want a drink?" Blair asks as she pushes her way through the crowd with her sights set on the bar.

"Yeah…" I attempt to take a steadying breath; there doesn't seem to be any oxygen in this room. It's hot. Too hot. Blair's head whips around and she looks at me with concern filling her eyes. Peeling my jacket down my arms in an attempt to cool off, I stumble; my balance is a little off.

"Shit, Em, you don't look too good," she says, taking my clammy arm and steering me over to a table so I can take a seat.

"I'll be okay, I swear."

"Yeah, I'm not buying that. What can I do? You want me to take you home?"

"NO!" It sounds desperate and I shake my head. Multi-colored spots float in front of Blair's face and I need to squint to bring her back into focus. "I promise I'm all right. The heat in here just got to me. Can you get me a bottle of water?"

"Don't move from here, okay? I'll go grab you one."

"Don't worry, I'll stay put." I attempt a reassuring smile, but by the look on her face, I failed. Good thing I left out the fact that I don't think I could stand without puking and passing out. I couldn't wander off even if I wanted to.

She frowns and then barges her way through the cramped club, like a tiny bulldozer. I love how fiercely she loves me. I can't think of a single thing she wouldn't do for me if I asked; friends like Blair are so rare. When she returns moments later with my water, I want to hug her tight and tell her what she means to me. But she'd probably think I was about to keel over and was attempting my last goodbye, so I hold back. I drink the water hoping it will make me feel better; it doesn't.

A guy comes out from behind the curtained area just off the tiny stage and introduces Kickstart. There's a huge gaggle of girls, some I even recognize from school, clamoring for a better spot next to the stage. When Jackson emerges and begins to fiddle with an amp, the club fills with whistles and cheers. The rest of the band walks out onto the stage and I crane my neck to try and get a better view. It's a hopeless effort as the dance floor floods with people and now I can only see a swarm of backs.

Ethan's voice fills the space around me as he introduces the band and their first song. I don't want to miss this; I've waited too long. I stand, ignoring the protests my body is making, and take a few tentative steps closer to the dance floor. I sway and Blair has me in an instant.

"Emily, I really think we need to go," she says in a soft voice in my ear. Her words are laced with sadness, just like my heart right now.

I twist to tell her no, but my vision takes a little longer to catch up with my body and I know I can't stay. I feel like my head is about to explode and I'm about ten seconds from internally combusting. I know she's right.

"Okay." I swallow the lump that's forming in my throat. Tonight was supposed to be so different. My chest tightens as the reality that Ethan Jamison and I are never going to happen sets in. The back of my eyes begins to sting, and I realize in horror a second too late that a tear has escaped.

Blair's face crumples. She takes a second to look at her feet before raising her head and offering me a smile I know she doesn't feel. "Let's get out of here."

I'm led out through the throng of people singing along to the music, and when I climb the three stairs to head out to the exit, I stop. Blair jolts back and I drop her hand as I look out over everyone's heads and take in the sight of Ethan. His eyes are closed as he sings into the microphone.

Enough. Enough is enough.

Blair takes my hand again and we leave. I'm hit with that feeling you get when you know you've misplaced something, or overlooked something important, only you can't quite remember what it is. But as Blair helps me into the car, I realize I do know what it is that I've forgotten.

My heart.

My broken heart that is sitting shattered at the table inside of the club.

ele

August 2nd, 2013

Dear Diary,

I want to give up. I'm not going to, but I want to. This shit's too hard.

ele

I haven't updated my diary in almost a week. I couldn't face it. I haven't been at school, either. Mom took me straight to the hospital on Friday night when Blair brought me home. After hooking me up to an IV for the evening to get some fluids into me, they let me leave Saturday morning with a bag full of meds and an appointment for Monday.

I haven't lived this week; I've only existed. And I'm sick to fuck of existing!

I pull on my sweater and head out to the car. My dad insisted on driving; maybe he thinks I'll ditch my appointment today. He's waiting to take me to Dr. Zahn's, and Blair's already sitting in the back seat. I don't know the exact moment we decided that she would come to my sessions with me, but I'm thankful she's here right now.

The ride to Dr. Zahn's office is painfully quiet. I'm not exactly in the mood to talk, and Dad and Blair seem to be taking their cues from me. The atmosphere is thick and muggy with everything that each of us isn't saying. Dad drops us at the entrance and I tell him not to wait. He looks sad as he puts the car in drive and pulls away.

"Seriously, Em… I can't even imagine how bad this is for you, but you have to pull yourself out of this funk. You really want to spend your time moping when we could be doing so much more? Let's go skydiving, or cliff jumping or something epic… Let's live."

My tears are instant, and by the look on Blair's face, completely unexpected.

"Shit …Gosh, Em, I didn't—"

"Stop! You're right. I just needed to hear it, I guess." I dig around in my purse, looking for something to dry my tears with, when Blair steps forward and swipes under my eyes with the sleeve of her shirt. "Nice!"

"Hey, you should be thankful. I love you, but damn, you are one ugly crier."

I burst out laughing because only she could say something so mean, yet project it with such good intentions. "Do I have panda eyes now?" I ask, widening them.

"A little bit, but it looks good. Kind of like you've tried to make your mascara all watery and smudged." I step back looking skeptically at her and she snorts. "Okay, maybe not good … but not horrendous."

"Great," I groan. "Well, let's go inside and get this over with. We don't want to be too late to go throw ourselves off a cliff!"

"Yeah … you do realize that I meant *you* should do that? Not me. I'll just watch and be there for, you know, moral support and stuff."

"Gee, thanks. Whatever happened to you go, I'll go?"

"Yeah, pretty sure I canned that after you convinced me to go to that roller skating rink last year. My ass has never seen so much floor time."

I loved that day. I spent more time helping her up off the floor than I did skating, but it was pure fun. Most things with Blair are.

We check in at reception, then wait to be called in. The blond guy with the slogan T-shirt is here again. He's leaning forward in one of the chairs reading a music magazine with a pair of obnoxiously large headphones on, bobbing his head to whatever's playing. I'm trying to peep over his magazine to see if he's wearing another slogan shirt. If he is, I'm totally introducing him to Blair. I turn to see she's pulled out her e-reader and is now mirroring the guy's pose, wearing her blue 'Free Shrugs' T-shirt.

"Yo man, done. Let's get outta here."

I twist and watch a stupidly hot guy with buzzed dark hair and a lip ring march towards us. His long-sleeved, gray henley is pulled deliciously tight over his slim yet muscular frame. My mouth is suddenly dry. Very, very dry.

Hot damn.

The T-shirt guy still hasn't looked up, so the hottie with the piercing slaps him across the head as he passes on the way to the exit. "Matt, come on!"

T-shirt guy, *Matt,* immediately rubs the spot and stands. He looks pissed. "Lucas, you dick, that hurt."

"Quit your bitching, little bro. I need to go." He looks back and catches me watching him. His lips quirk ever so slightly before he turns again and disappears out the exit. That smirk, his lip ring … I'm pretty sure my ovaries have just exploded. *Wow.*

Matt throws down his magazine and heads out, trailing his brother. I spin to make eyes at Blair about how yummy the brothers are, and she's reading away, oblivious. I don't think she's even heard the exchange. "Did you just see how hot those two were?" I ask in a dreamy voice.

"Huh? What two?" she asks, not looking away from her e-reader.

"How could you not have noticed them?" I drop backwards dramatically and she finally looks at me and shrugs. "What the hell are you reading that has you glued to that thing?" It's more a rhetorical question, but suddenly she's all animated and alert.

"Oh, it's so good. It's this book about this deaf guy who's a songwriter and so swoon-worthy and this girl who's helping him and they…" she trails off when she sees my expression. "What's funny?"

"Swoon-worthy?"

"Oh, shut up. He's hot!"

"No, the two guys you just missed in *here* were hot, but you were too immersed in your fictional boyfriend there."

She scowls and is about to shoot some smart-ass retort, no doubt, when my name's called to go through.

"Saved." I grin. "Be back soon."

"Take your time," she fires back as she picks up her e-reader and carries on lusting after her book boyfriend.

Maybe that's where I'm going wrong. I shouldn't be lusting after Ethan; I should be engrossing myself in perfect fictional boys, and get my hits that way. Let's face it; Ethan may as well be fictional. The way things are panning out; I have about as much chance with him as I do with Mr. Darcy.

7

August 10th, 2013

Dear Diary,

Turns out getting insurance for a terminally ill girl for any type of extreme sport is about as easy as extracting blood from a stone. It seems every company in California is hung up on the whole cancer thing. No one is willing to let me participate in case I croak on 'their time'. I get it, but it sucks.

ele

Blair left after we spent three hours online searching for cancer-friendly extreme sports. She looked more defeated than me. Instead, I've talked her into accompanying me while I get a tattoo. She's coming with me Monday after school to go check out some shops. I'm equal parts excited and terrified, but I like the feeling. I head through the house looking for my parents so I can prep them on the idea, and fall short of their room as I hear the conversation going on inside.

My dad seems to be comforting my mom while she cries about how this is the wrong way around. They should be the ones to die first. I lean against the wall beside their room, careful to keep out of sight. Mom isn't holding back now; she's full-on sobbing and hiccuping while telling Dad that they'll never see me in a wedding dress. *Like he hasn't figured this out yet for himself.*

My stomach plummets to the floor and I shift from one foot to another. The floorboards creak and I dart back to my room before they give me away. I paint my nails to try and distract myself until I hear cupboards opening and closing in the kitchen. I'm assuming it means they've both pulled themselves together enough to risk seeing me, so I make my way through.

"Where's Dad?" I ask as I watch Mom pull a packet of coffee from the back of the cupboard.

"He's gone for a run, sweetie," she says matter-of-factly before throwing me a smile. Mom's got a great game face. If I'd not overheard her conversation, I'd have no clue she was just upset.

"Okay, I have an idea, and I want you to just trust me, so grab your things and come with me. We're going out."

Mom looks a little bewildered by my cryptic request before she shrugs and grins. "Fine, lead the way, Emily."

We climb into her car and I scroll through my phone until I find the address of the nearest bridal store. I locate one three miles away and begin inputting it into the GPS. Mom looks at the address, and I can see the gears in her head turning as she tries to work out the address and wonders what would have me dragging her out the house for.

She's a good sport and doesn't seem too put out that I'm refusing to tell her what it is we're doing as we make the short journey.

A few minutes roll by before we pull up outside Dana's Bridal Boutique, and the GPS signals that we've reached our destination on the left. Mom looks at me questioningly and I give her a rueful smile. There's only a bakery, coffee shop and the bridal store on this small stretch of road.

"I overheard you and Dad talking this morning." She still looks confused so I point to the Bridal Boutique. She covers her mouth with her hand as she leans back into her seat, her eyes crinkling as realization dawns. "You were talking about the fact that you should go first, and that you'll never see me in my wedding dress, or be there with me at the delivery of your first grandchild. Well, there's little I can do about an immaculate conception," I shrug, "but this," I point to the store again. "This I can do."

I watch as a million different emotions wage war behind her sapphire eyes before she admits defeat, closes them tightly and slumps forward resting her elbows on her knees and her head in her hands. I watch quietly as she holds a finger up to me, signaling she needs a minute. When she finally opens them again, they're glassy but she seems to have recovered her composure enough to step outside the car. I don't know what to make of the situation, and honestly, I'm regretting my decision as I climb out and round the car. Maybe this was a stupid idea and is too much for her. Hell, maybe it's too much for me. I'm about to apologize and tell her so when she finally speaks.

"You really are something kind of wonderful, Emily," she says before ambushing me in a fiercely tight hug. I sigh and feel a little of the tension drain from my shoulders, like someone's just turned on an invisible faucet to ease some of the pressure.

"I'm sorry you heard that conversation. I was just having a weak moment. We don't have to do this," she whispers into my hair and squeezes before pushing me back to see my face.

"I'm glad I did hear, and I want to do this. Is that weird?" I answer, and it's the truth. I *am* glad I overheard their conversation. I hate that she feels like she needs to be strong one hundred percent of the time for me. It's not healthy.

"It's not weird at all, Emily."

"Good. Okay, enough of this." I square my shoulders. "Let's get in there and go play dress up."

A bell sounds as we enter the store and I almost pee my pants at the unexpected shrill of it. Mom laughs as she ushers me through and we shuffle further into the room. It's fancier that I was expecting. The whole place is whitewashed except for the dark cherry wood floors. Huge crystal chandeliers hang from the ceilings, and there are multiple seating areas, with velvet couches and large standing silver candelabras.

"Hello."

A beautiful lady with reddish hair and huge black hipster glasses like Blair's barrels towards us under a mass of cream-colored lace and tulle. I pause because I haven't really thought this through. *Like, at all.* I figure I have two options at the moment: lie and tell her I'm planning my wedding, or the truth, even though that will be all kinds of awkward. The lady deposits the mound of fabric onto one of the chairs we're standing by, fishing out a hanger and shaking the whole thing a few times. As if by magic, the material transforms into a beautifully intricate lace gown before us. She smiles, running her hand over the skirt and then hangs the gown on a little silver hook.

"Beautiful, isn't it? It's imported Chantilly lace. We just had it delivered."

Mom sighs beside me. "It's magnificent," she replies and the lady beams at her.

"So, ladies, do you have an appointment?"

"You need an appointment to try a wedding dress on?" I mutter to myself, bemused.

"Of course, I can book you in right now if you'd like," she asks, pulling an enormous cream leather appointment book from under the counter. She begins leafing through the pages. "I know I have an opening, ah, here it is. How about three weeks from today?" she says, looking up over the rim of her glasses.

Shit, it's possible that I might not even be here in three weeks. I swallow the thought like an acrid pill, and it leaves a foul taste in my mouth. Well, I guess this solves my little conundrum about what tact to take. There's only one way forward; I'm going to have to tell her the truth. As much as I hate playing the cancer card, I'm pretty sure it will be my only chance at getting to try anything on today.

"Oh, I'm sorry—" Mom begins, but I cut her short.

"The thing is, Miss—"

"Please, call me Dana."

"Oh, um, the thing is, Dana, I have kind of a unique situation here."

I proceed to tell her about my prognosis, and what it is that we're doing here and why. "So you see, I know it's a lot to ask and I'd completely understand if—"

Dana stands from the little couch that she's been sitting on since I basically blindsided her and waves her hands in the air. "Sweetheart, I've heard all I need to hear," she says, pulling out a tissue from a little silver box beside the couch, and wiping her nose. "I have a client booked in just over an hour for a final fitting. I know that's not much time, but it would truly be my pleasure to help you."

My mom thanks her and passes her another tissue before she leads us through the store and into what can only be described as a dress closet on steroids.

ele

We spend a few minutes overwhelmed by all the dresses before Dana pulls out a pure white, silk Vera Wang strapless gown with a sweetheart neckline. It's strikingly simple, except for the thin, light blue sash that ties in a neat little bow on my hip. If I actually were getting married, I have no doubts I would be begging my dad for this dress.

It's perfect.

"Here, just slip those on and I'll be in to strap you up in just a second," Dana says, offloading a pair of white satin pumps. They have a gazillion tiny crystals shimmering from the heels and are off-the-charts beautiful. I clutch them to my chest, trying to keep the gown I'm half-wearing from slipping down. She's back holding what I'm assuming is a veil before I even have a chance to adjust my stance. Mom's patiently sitting in the viewing area, awaiting my entrance.

"Okay, sweetheart, time to suck it in," Dana warns before pulling the corset at the back of the dress so tight that I might actually faint. I'm pretty sure my circulation has been cut off from the waist down after she finishes manipulating my body into a perfect hourglass. It's about as comfy as a G-string fashioned out of razor blades, but it looks incredible.

"Final touch," she says, taking the floor-length veil that's attached to a crystal clip and pushing it gently into my short hair. I'm thankful now that I took the time to put a little product in it this morning, with my attempt at a messy-beach hair style, or there's no way the veil would stay.

"Wow, I had no idea that I could ever look like this," I say, swaying the dress from side to side and marveling at my reflection. "Thank you, so, so much for this."

My throat feels tight and I'm unexpectedly filled with emotion. I don't want to cry, but I know if I blink right now the tears will come.

"You, my dear, are one of the prettiest brides I think I've ever had the pleasure of dressing," Dana states with a warm, affectionate smile. It does nothing to dissolve the lump forming in my throat.

Suddenly, the reality of what's happening hits me like a sucker punch to the gut. I'm sure it would knock me down if I actually had the ability to bend in this dress. I'm never getting married.

I'm never buying a house or fighting with my partner about what color blinds to hang in the bedroom.

I'll never have a proud mother moment when my child takes his or her first steps.

It's not fair!

I'm a good person; I deserve those things, or at least I deserve a shot at them. Don't I?

"Emily, are you ready to show your mom?" she asks, oblivious to the internal freak out I'm experiencing, and it breaks me out of my own thoughts. I take a deep breath ... well, what was supposed to be deep. It's more of a shallow wheeze since I'm pretty sure my lungs have been relocated after trying on this gown.

"You think I could have just a second, please?"

I'm answered with a small knowing nod as she re-treats back around the curtain and I hear her strike up a conversation with Mom. I allow myself thirty seconds of mourning for the life I'll never have, and then put my game face back on. If I'm going to leave my mom with a memory of this, then it damn well better be a good one.

Chapter 8

August 12th, 2013

Dear Diary,

I've had what you could term a surreal weekend. I spent Saturday trying on wedding dresses with my mom. It was one of those moments that restore your faith in humanity. Dad always has the news playing in the background, wherever he is, and it's always filled with god-awful stories. People being murdered, terrorism, financial meltdowns, and natural disasters. Do the television networks have some sort of no-happiness clause where they're not allowed to report on anything good? So yeah, in a world where you're constantly exposed to shitty things, this act of kindness really touched me. Dana not only let us try on dresses, she let Mom take pictures, too, which is apparently against company policy. It was an emotional experience, but I have to admit, it was nice, even if a little bittersweet.

Sunday was hilarious, and it's all due to Blair, Casey, and Brie. We arranged to meet for coffee and basically spent hours putting the world to rights and indulging in mindless gossip. It was great to feel healthy and carefree for a few hours. We were huddled in the far corner of The Grind, a small mom and pop store on the end of Main. It's Brie's new fascination; the coffee is excellent, but that's not what has her driving past three different coffee franchises to get here. The new barista is smoking hot. Even though he's not my type, I can still appreciate that he's gorgeous.

When we noticed that he was working, Brie immediately volunteered as tribute! She never offers to get the coffee, so Blair, Casey and I all looked at each other like maybe we'd heard her wrong. She smirked and told us to watch and learn how to snare a guy in two minutes flat. The girl is the epitome of confidence, so we each made ourselves comfy for the show. She sashayed to the counter like she was walking the runway. Casey was muttering loud enough for just about everyone in the place to hear, "Work it, work it, baby, own it," a la Kit from "Pretty Woman." Blair and I were laughing through our cupped hands, and Brie snapped her head back to shoot us 'the look.'

All her ass swaying weighed against her though. Literally! She carried on walking as she looked back to scowl at us and didn't see that Barista Babe had moved around the counter with a tray of iced coffees for a group sitting by the window. One minute she's like a panther stalking her prey, and the next, she's teetering on her heels from the exaggerated ass swaying and is barreling towards the coffee god. I swear, it was like slow motion watching as the tray flipped, she landed, and then found herself taking a Frappuccino bath in the middle of the store.

Blair shot up to go help as Casey and I were pinned to our seats with belly crunching laughter. Brie was shrieking about how freezing the drinks were while trying to hold her shirt away from her skin. Barista Babe looked confused. It was like he couldn't work out what just happened. He stood staring at Brie floundering about in a pool of coffee, like a kid who had just dove into the deep end of the pool before realizing he couldn't swim.

By this time, Blair was bending down to collect Brie from the floor. At the same time, the guy finally managed to work out that he could move. He turned to help her just as Blair lifted her, and the back of her head made an impressive crunch against his nose. They both cursed in unison as Casey and I watched in morbid fascination. They immediately clasped their respective hurts, and Barista Babe paced around in a tiny circle with his head tilted forward as the blood began to drip.. Blair was still rubbing the back of her head but rooted to the spot as she muttered a nervous apology, and Brie was still sitting in a puddle of coffee. The older man who works the till rounded the corner with a handful of tissue and thrust some at the coffee god while dropping the rest to the floor to soak up the mess.

The whole event couldn't have lasted more than two minutes, tops, but every time I think about it, I laugh my ass off. We left shortly after Brie returned from the restroom, where she'd attempted to dry her shirt under the hand blowers. She stopped at the counter on our way out to apologize to the Barista Babe, who was leaned against the back wall with two wads of tissue pushed up his nostrils to cap the flow of blood. His eyes were already starting to blacken and the "Don't worry about it, accidents happen," comment he threw at her didn't really match the scowl on his face.

Undeterred by disaster, Brie decided it was the perfect opportunity to ask him out. She mumbled something along the lines of, "Let me make it up to you. We can grab a drinks some time ... my treat?" The guy's eyebrows shot straight to his hairline in surprise and by the wince the look turned into, I could tell the movement hurt. There was a really awkward long silence as she waited for a reply. The poor guy must have been intimidated, as me, Blair and Casey stood behind Brie—all watching the interaction. Don't judge me, I have kind of a sick fascination with watching awkward moments play out. They're like car crashes that you know you shouldn't look at, but you just can't summon the strength to pull your gaze away.

The guy shifted from foot to foot and then politely declined, saying he was flattered, but she wasn't really his type. Brie being Brie, she drawls out in a sickly sweet voice that has the rest of us sniggering like the schoolgirls we are, "Sweetheart, I'm everyone's type." She says it so matter-of-fact, that if it were anyone else, it would have sounded completely conceited. Somehow she pulled it off without sounding like a douche.

The guy looked her square in the eyes, seemingly ready to decline her for a second time, then smiled and shook his head. He let out another wince and what sounded like "fuck" under his breath before answering her again. Only it's not what any of us were expecting. In fact, even Brie looked a little shocked. He told her to meet him at seven after his shift on Wednesday and then disappeared into the back room.

Casey bumped shoulders with Brie and looked genuinely in awe. Blair leaned over to me and whispered, "Dude, am I missing something here? How did that just happen? We just totaled the store and, by the looks of it, broke his nose, and he still agreed to go on a date with her?"

"Oh, my gosh, look at the state of me!" Brie shrieked as we exited The Grind. She'd pulled her cell out of her purse to check her reflection in the camera. "I look like I've been mud wrestling and lost!"

"Hence, the reason why you now have a date Wednesday," Case replied with a grin.

I shook my head in confusion because, after all that she'd still seized the moment. She took a leap of faith and put herself out there. She even did it with an audience for Christ's sake, and it paid off. I need to rip a page out of her book.

Carpe diem!

Chapter 9

HOLY SHIT, THIS was a bad idea.

"Blair, I think I'm having second thoughts," I whisper shout over the buzz of the gun in the cubicle at the back of the store.

"What? No way, you can't back out now! You've made me wait for hours while you've been looking through those books!" she whines and I let my shoulders drop. It's true; she's not even exaggerating. We've been in here two hours, and the longer we've been here, the more grown men I've seen leave with unshed tears in their eyes. *Crap.*

"Emily?"

The guy rounds the cubicle and I'm filled with an overwhelming urge to run. Blair grabs my wrist just as I decide to make a play for the door.

"Here she is!" Blair shouts to Manzilla, and if I didn't love her so much, I'm pretty sure I'd punch her.

"Thanks, friend," I grind out, trying not to display my nerves too much. I stand and drag her up with me.

"Dude, I said I'd come with you, but I can't watch

while they stick you with needles. I'll faint!"

"Since when have you had a problem with needles?" I ask as I take slow, tentative steps towards the hulking mountain of a guy who's now disappeared behind the cubicle again, coaxing her with me.

"I don't have a problem with needles. I have a problem with blood. And, Em, did you not see that guy who just left? He'd been crying, no doubt about it. His eyes were all puffy and stuff."

"Thanks for that. You're *not* actually making me feel better about this!"

"Sorry," she says sheepishly. "I'm sure you'll be fine. Women have a stronger pain threshold than men. That's why we're they ones that suffer childbirth." She shrugs and I laugh.

"Did you just make that up?"

"No, I'm serious. If guys had to go through it, they'd extinct themselves within a decade!"

"Valid point." I stop and turn to her. "Please come with me? That dude's scary," I plead and she sighs and concedes. We round the corner and the guy gestures for me to take a seat on the big leather dentist-type chair.

"Take a seat over there, Tiny," he says to Blair, pointing to a stool by the mirror. She throws me a look that lets me know she finds how he addressed her amusing. Blair's not tall, but she's hardly tiny. Then again, this guy looks to be at least six and a half feet tall; most people probably seem small to him. He's built like a UFC fighter. Massive! The skin stretched over his bulging muscles from the bottom of his T-shirt sleeves to the beginning of his blue latex gloves is adorned with a million and one brightly-colored tattoos. They all blend seamlessly into one another. He's like walking art.

The cubicle reminds me of the hospital; it smells of alcohol wipes. It's brilliant white and sterile, apart from some pretty sick drawings that have been framed with thick black acrylic and rest on a floating white shelf.

"Okay, I'm Gus. Star tells me you're off treatment and want to get inked?" he says, looking over the paperwork that I'd handed back to the receptionist after spending an eternity filling out.

"Yeah," is all I can manage to answer through the nerves closing up my throat.

"Your immune system back to normal?" he asks, looking up from the clipboard.

"Nope," I say and smile weakly. "My neutrophil levels are high enough for this not to be a problem, though," I quickly add. "I actually have a copy of my last blood count saved to my emails on my phone if you need to see them. As long as you're reputable and everything's sterile, I shouldn't keel over and die on you," I say with a wink, trying to alleviate some of the tension in the room.

He laughs. "Okay, well, you don't mince your words. Shit. You know what you want?"

"Yeah, but I couldn't find anything in your books that incorporates it completely. I want something that means life goes on. I was thinking of a silhouette of a tree, like this one," I show him the picture in his book. "But I want to fuse it into a circle, you know, like the circle of life? Does that make sense?"

He smiles, seemingly impressed with my choice. "It does, although I'd have bet my bike that you were in here for another fucking butterfly. What is it with chicks and butterflies?" he asks with a grin, and I decide I like him. Even if he does look like he could tear me apart with his pinky finger.

"Right." I giggle nervously and Blair snorts.

"I love that you just said that! She wanted a butterfly until she saw the tree," Blair tells him and I feel the heat in my cheeks rise instantly. I spin around and she's wearing the biggest shit-eating grin. I want to throw the tub of Vaseline that's sitting next to me at her, but I can't because she's telling the truth.

I assumed that getting a tattoo would be a touch on the uncomfortable side; I'd already prepped myself for the fact that it wasn't going to tickle. *But holy hell does it hurt!* My first clue that this was going to be about as much fun as Chinese water torture should have been when I said I wanted the tat on my ribs, just under my left breast, and Gus whistled. I thought he was whistling because… Well, if I'm being honest, because he thought it was hot. But no, it was to signify that if you're going to get a tattoo anywhere, your ribs are about the most painful place you can choose. The tattoo gun had barely warmed before I was reciting the periodic table song in my mind to try and take my mind off the fact that I'm actually paying him to hurt me this much. I quickly run out of stupid things to recite and look over to Blair, hoping she can keep me occupied. She's facing away with her hands cupped over her ear as she stares at the ground.

"Blair, what are you doing?" I shout.

She answers without moving an inch. "I can't look. And the sound … damn, it's worse than the drill they use at the dentist. Just shout at me when you're done." She shudders.

Gus lets out a low rumbling sound, which I'm assuming is a laugh.

"Bet you wish all your customers were as mentally stable as us," I say sarcastically through gritted teeth as he drags the tattoo needle across my sensitive skin. It feels like he's burning me rather than piercing the skin with a needle.

"Trust me, you two are a walk in the park. We get some … let's call them *interesting* people in here."

"Feel free to tell me about them to take my mind off this torture."

There he goes again with the rumbling laugh. "Last week this couple came in, I guess around your age, maybe a little older," he begins. "The chick is all hyped up and says, 'Hey, I'd like to get a tattoo of my boyfriend's name, but I'm scared of needles. Is there anything you can do? So I say, 'Well, not really. We could try cooling cream first. It would numb the skin a little but not totally.' It's pretty normal for us to get people coming in who don't like needles. I mean fuck, unless you're a junkie, who does? So anyway, the chick's like, 'Huh, yeah, no, I don't think so. Just show me the needles. I'll faint, and then you can do the name while I'm out,' like that's an entirely normal request." He rolls his eyes.

He says the female customer's part in a high-pitched girly voice, which coming out of him is so weird and completely hilarious I can't help but grin.

"I tell her that I think that's probably illegal but she's already walked over to my table and picked up a needle, still in its steri-wrapper. I go to take it off her and before I get there, she's opened the packaging, then boom—she's flat-out cold on the tile floor. I grab my phone to call for an ambulance because this chick didn't faint like a girl. She hit the deck like a sack of rocks, and then get this." He stops tattooing me for a second to look at me. "Her douche of a boyfriend turns to me and says, 'Dude, can't you just do it now?' I'm looking at him, standing there with his girl decked out, thinking *is this guy for real*."

"Oh my gosh. Was the girl all right?" I ask, trying not to laugh.

"I think so. The EMT's took her to the hospital as a precaution since she'd banged her head." He shrugs and then starts the gun up again, pressing it back to my skin. "Her dickhead boyfriend was pissed at me for calling them because it was going to make him late for some basketball game or something. The dude was lucky he didn't end up in the back of the ambulance, too." He smirks.

"There we go," Gus says, sliding away from me on his roller chair to look over his handy work. "I'm impressed, Emily. Most grown men I tattoo on the ribs don't sit as still as you just did. 'Though she be but little, she is fierce.'" He winks.

"Wow, did you just quote Shakespeare to me?" I ask, failing miserably at masking the surprise in my voice. Gus doesn't look like your average 1600's playwright aficionado.

"You sound surprised. Anyone ever tell you not judge a book by its cover, Emily? You might miss out on a great story."

"Oh, um, I didn't mean to offend you—"

"Relax, I'm not offended. I'm majoring in English lit, so I spent all last semester reading Shakespeare."

"Holy crap, you're still in college?" I blurt out.

"Okay, now I'm offended!" He laughs.

"Oh, no, sorry, I'm just shocked. I thought you were older—"

"Keep digging, sweetheart."

"Gee, Em, you're acting almost as awkward as me!" Blair chimes in, and I look over wide-eyed, silently willing the floor to open up and swallow me.

"I'm twenty-three. Guess it's time to break out the anti-wrinkle cream already, huh?" Gus says playfully. "Stand up and take a look." He points at the tattoo and I grin, eager to see what it looks like.

"Wow." I turn to my side and look at my reflection in the mirror. "It's perfect."

"Again with the surprise." He shakes his head. "You'll give a guy a complex."

"It was most definitely a compliment, Gus. Thank you."

"Um, is that all blood?" Blair asks, pointing to the trashcan filled with the tissues that he's used while inking me.

"What? There's hardly anything there. Ribs barely bleed," Gus answers.

"Yeah, it's enough. I need some air … I'll be outside, Em." Suddenly, she's gone.

"Tiny wasn't joking when she told you she doesn't do blood well, huh?"

"Apparently not." I smile. "Okay, so do I just pay on the way out?" I ask as he tapes me up and hands me a leaflet on how to take care of my new ink.

"You know what? It's on me."

"What? No way. You can't," I say dismissively.

"Sure I can, just smile and say thank you."

"No, really. I don't mean to be disrespectful or anything, but I don't like feeling like I pulled the cancer card. I'll pay—"

"Seriously, you're not pulling anything. It's on me because you impressed me with how badass you are—not even flinching as I worked on your ribs. I've made two dudes cry today tattooing theirs." He smiles. It's so genuine that I don't dare turn him down again.

"Wow, thank you then, I guess."

"You're welcome, Emily. See you around," he says softly.

I don't have the heart to tell him that it's highly unlikely he'll ever see me again, so I don't. "See you around, Gus." I catch the look he gives me as I round the cubicle to leave.

He knows.

Chapter 10

August 24th, 2013

Dear Diary,

Eat. Sleep. Rinse. Repeat.

I'm sure I've ended up stuck in some weird time loop for the last week. You know, like the movie "Groundhog Day" where you live the same day over and over.

I feel sorry for myself today.

When I was at Dr. Zahn's she told me that it sounded to her like I was in the grieving stages of my diagnosis. I asked her what it was that I was supposed to be grieving, because grief happens when you lose someone, and I'm not dead … yet. And when I am, I can't exactly mourn myself. She shook her head and smiled at me before sitting back in her chair. Her demeanor was relaxed and not at all like a therapist taking notes. She made me feel like we were just hanging out and talking like old friends.

She began telling me that grief is an overwhelming emotion, regardless of whether your sadness comes from experiencing a physical loss or from a terminal diagnosis like mine. Apparently it's normal—expected, even—that I might feel numb and disconnected from my friends, family, or life in general. She asked me if I felt like I was unable to continue with my everyday, regular routines. My first instinct was to say no. It's not like I'm having suicidal thoughts and don't want to carry on. If anything, it's the opposite; I don't want anything to end. I told her this, and she said that's not what she meant.

"Are you having the 'what's the point' feelings every time you do anything?"

I don't exactly think, 'what's the point' because, for me, the point is to live. But I am tiring of things, my emotions are all over the place, and I'm back on pretty heavy-duty pain medication. As much as I hate to admit it, I do feel like maybe I'm just waiting to die. I don't want to be that person. I don't want to sit and let death claim me. I want to be that girl who dies doing something epic; not in a hospital bed, off my face on drugs. When I said this to her, she hugged me. I'm pretty sure that's not normal patient/therapist protocol, but I think we've bypassed that now.

She finished by telling me that grief is the natural reaction to an impending loss. That it's a very personal experience, and that even though I may not be in control of the ultimate outcome, I am in charge of the journey. She's an extraordinary person, Dr. Zahn. She inspires me.

I'm in charge of my own journey.

I like that.

I walk into my bedroom with a towel wrapped like a turban around my head.

"Is it done?" Blair asks, looking up from my desk chair. She's been helping me catch up on my homework.

I beam. "It is."

She stands, stretching and contorting her spine in an exaggerated arch like a lazy cat awakening from a long nap. She'd turned up a few hours ago in denim shorts and a red plaid shirt. I greeted her in the kitchen dressed in my own denim shorts and a blue plaid shirt. Dad shook his head and asked if we called each other in the morning so that we could coordinate properly. Mom nudged him and told him that we're like those twins who have telepathic abilities. Dad shivered dramatically and looked at us both like we were creeping him out.

"Are we scaring you?" we both said in unison, and Dad spit the OJ he was drinking back into his glass, looking at us with eyes as large as saucers. "Jinx, double jinx! You get the pinch I get the wish!" we shouted, facing one another and then attempting to nip each other's arms.

"You weren't scaring me, but now you are." He'd left the room, still looking back at the two of us like we're unsettling him.

"Ignore him, girls. He spends too much time watching the paranormal channel," Mom mused before picking up her coffee and retreating after Dad.

"We do have a knack for coming off as similar," Blair said. So, after we'd finished studying, I pulled the dye I'd bought at the drug store out and told her I was going to change things up a little.

And here I am, poised and ready for my reveal.

"Are you going to show me or not? Wait—does it look bad? Is that why you're stalling? We can always fix it, you know. I'll drive you to a salon—you can wear a baseball cap and hoodie. We'll don shades and go on a covert mission!"

"Easy, tiger. I think you're getting way ahead of yourself. I was pausing for dramatic effect, but you've kind of killed it!" I smirk.

"Oh for…" she shakes her head, exasperated. "Just show me already!"

"Ta daaaa," I sing-song as I pull the towel from around my head and reveal my hair.

"Emily!" Blair's eyes are huge and I smile. "Is it supposed to be pink?"

"What, no!" I joke and her expression is priceless. I grab a pillow from my bed and toss it at her. "Of course it's supposed to be pink. Nobody, not even me, can dye her hair—what did it say on the box? oh, yeah—'Foxy Fuchsia,' by mistake."

"It's mega bright! Like I think I need to switch out my glasses for my shades." She grins and I perch on the end of my bed laughing. "What made you decide to color your hair pink? I thought you were in there putting a few highlights in it."

"Why not pink? I just wanted to do something different for once." I don't add that it's on my bucket list because … well, because she still doesn't know about that. I've checked off the tattoo and now I can put a check next to this, too.

"With your hair in that pixy cut, you look like a sexed-up version of Tinker Bell on steroids! It's cool though. You're owning it."

"Um …Thanks." *I think?*

"Are you keeping it like that for the winter formal?" she asks, sitting beside me on my bed.

Damn, I hadn't thought of that. My face contorts into a grimace and she instantly begins to laugh. Blair has the best laugh ever; she has no control over it and involuntarily snorts. It's hilarious.

"You forgot, then," she states rather than asks and I fall back with my hands over my face.

"Yep … I got a little while though, right? When is it?"

"You have two weeks," she confirms.

"Oh, that's not so bad," I reply, sitting back up. I can be blonde by then … I think.

"You could keep it that color. It would look great contrasting against the blue of your dress."

"Nope, I have a plan and a firm vision in my head of how I need to look that night, to pull it off." She raises her brows, waiting for me to clarify, but I don't. Instead, I grin and then hop up off the bed. "Come on, let's go make popcorn and watch a movie. I'll make you a milkshake," I offer.

"You had me at popcorn. Plus," she pauses for effect, "I wouldn't miss your folks' reaction to your hair for the world, I need popcorn just to witness that." I roll my eye but laugh in spite of myself. I should grab my cell so I can take a picture.

This should be fun.

Who knew that store bought permanent hair color was actually permanent? Not me, that's for sure. I had edgy, cool, bright pink hair for a week. Then I tried to dye it blonde and ended up with aluminous orange. You know, the color of prison jumpsuits. I rocked the pink. The orange? Not so much. Blair said if you dressed me in a pair of denim overalls, I'd look like Chucky from that slasher movie. Dad thought it was hilarious and actually high-fived her. *Assholes.*

Mom drove me to the salon this morning and Hayley, the hairdresser, took one look at me and flinched. I'm currently sitting under the dryer with my head saran wrapped. I feel like a freaking hors-d'oeuvre about to be slapped onto a platter and offered out to one and all. The little buzzer Hayley had set begins a jarring shriek beside my ear. I have no escape from the shrillness; the dome dryer is acting as a soundboard and I can feel everyone's eyes on me, waiting for the horrendous noise to be dealt with. Hayley saunters over with a broad grin and peels back some of the saran wrap, prodding at my head with the end of her comb. She sucks the air in through her teeth and I tense my shoulders in panic.

"This is going to need a bit longer," she says, patting the plastic film back in place with all the finesse of a blind drunk. She presses so hard, I slink back into my seat and she chuckles, pulling me forward. "Careful, sugar, you been drinking or something?" she says jokingly, as I sit with my mouth gaping open.

Seriously?

She leans in close enough that I can smell the cherry lip gloss she's wearing and whispers, "I had a few cheeky glasses of wine last night myself. Hell of a hangover this morning. You want to try a hair of the dog? It'll fix you right up." She flips her long blonde hair and walks away to tend to another client.

I'm too stunned to form a reply. That's all I need—a ditzy, half-wasted woman bleaching my hair before the formal. This can't end well.

Shit.

My head is starting to tingle, which I'm pretty damn sure is a bad thing. I look around the salon from my seat— the same seat I've been in for what feels like hours. I'm contemplating getting up and rinsing this crap off myself when Hayley walks back.

"Okay, sugar, let's get you over to the basins," she drawls and I'm mentally thanking God that she's not leaving me under the dryer any longer. The ceiling above the basins is mirrored, and I watch in horror as the peroxide cocktail I've been smothered in washes away, leaving almost-white hair in its wake.

Hayley must notice the look of sheer panic that's painted on my features and giggles—actually giggles. Like leaving me looking like some sort of albino rat in a drug trial is acceptable. "Relax, Emily. I have to add toner to it yet."

Thank fuck. The bright orange Chucky hair looked way better than this.

I close my eyes and don't look again as she massages what I'm assuming is the toner into my hair. She's regaling me with a story of how she once dyed her own hair black when she was younger, and immediately hated it. Because she's naturally a very light blonde, she researched how to return it to its natural color on the Internet. Apparently, the forum she'd sourced her information from wasn't such a great authority on hair care. Someone had posted that if she washed her hair in Pine-Sol, it would strip back the color. So she did! Not only did it NOT work, it made her hair indigo and she smelled like a forest for the next two weeks. I'm glad she can laugh as she's telling me this because it's disguising me hyperventilating over the fact that I've let this crazy woman anywhere near me.

Chapter 11

IT'S T-MINUS ONE hour and counting until West Point High's senior winter formal.

"So, how do I look?" I ask, twirling around in front of my bedroom mirror. I'm wearing the midnight blue, floor-length strapless gown that I bought with Mom. The dark material is a much starker contrast to my pale skin than I first envisioned it would be. I think maybe my HB levels are low; I'm sure I didn't look this pallid the last time I tried the dress on. I'm almost halfway through my six-month life expectancy and today, for the first time, I feel like it may be starting to show.

"You look amazing," Blair answers with a smile. "If you were ever going to make a play for Ethan Jamison, you should do it in that dress."

"You know what? I think tonight may be the night. This is most likely going to be the last winter formal I attend. I'm making the most of it."

She attempts a weak smile as my words register and I instantly feel bad for making her sad. Today has been a good day, and I'm hoping tonight will be even better, so I want my best friend happy and on form.

"Let's go down and let your mom and dad take a billion photos so we can get out of here," she replies.

"Wait, I need to fix my hair!" I tell her with a hint of amusement to my lilt. As it happens, Hayley has done an excellent job on my hair. It's not exactly the same as my natural color, but it's pretty damn close. I lick the palm of my hand, smooth it across my head and wiggle my eyebrows, smirking. "Done!"

Blair rolls her eyes and shakes her head in amusement. I know she's jealous; it only takes me two-seconds to style my own hair. She had to endure forty minutes of teasing and coiffuring with a shit ton of bobby pins and enough hairspray to be labeled the sole instigator in the problem with the ozone layer. Blair walks ahead of me in her green, fifties-style prom dress as we make our way through the house. It's only seconds before we're bombarded by camera flashes.

"You two look beautiful," Dad tells us, peeking up from behind his camera lens.

"Thanks, Bill," Blair grins before he lunges into the obligatory curfew and 'stay safe, don't drink and drive, be careful' talk. We're finally allowed out of the door after my Mom gushes over how pretty we look and poses between us for a few more shots.

ele

We arrive at the school gym, which has been decorated in mounds of silver and white sparkly tinsel; it's like Christmas threw up a few months early. Fake snow has been laid out, and snowflake decorations cover every available surface in sight. I'm feeling a little lightheaded, and I'm really hoping it's just the excitement and rushing about we've been doing. I grab Blair's hand and head straight to the dance floor. I love to dance; it's so freeing. Blair's not big on it, although she has great rhythm. I think she just lacks the confidence to let herself go completely and let the music take over.

We dance for at least six songs, but I can feel myself dizzying. I stop and stumble as Blair reaches for my arm. "Shit, are you okay?" she asks.

"Yeah, I'm fine. I just need to sit down, I think. I'm a little dizzy."

She immediately links her arm through mine and guides me to one of the bench seats that line the perimeter of the room. We sit down, watching the crowd as I concentrate on taking deep calming breaths. *Inhale, exhale, inhale, exhale …* Don't do this, I plead with my body. Don't fail me yet.

"You feel better now?"

"Yeah, a little bit. I guess I just overdid it," I answer as I look up and notice Ethan Jamison walking towards the halls. *Okay, this is it.*

"You know what, Blair? I'm gonna make a move. He can only say no, right?"

Her smile is huge as she nods in agreement. "Definitely!"

It's all the encouragement I need. I stand and smooth my dress down, ready to go and make my play on the guy that I've fantasized about for so long now. *Even if things do go well, how could they ever match what I've built up in my head?* I give the thought all of two seconds before shaking it off and decide that I need to find out.

I don't know what's going on.

I'm on the floor and Blair looks terrified. I can taste the metallic tang of blood on my lips and raise my hand to my face before realizing that my nose is gushing with blood.

"Em, Jesus … Are you okay? Your body just went limp and before I could catch you, you'd collapsed on the floor in front of me," she says in one long shuddering breath.

I want to reply, but I'm choking on the blood that's now filling the back of my throat.

𝓮𝓵𝓮

It was one of the teachers who called the ambulance that has transported us to the hospital. This whole night feels like a blur. One minute I'm on a manhunt for Ethan, and the next thing I know, I'm sitting in the Teenage Cancer Unit common room with Blair, hooked up to an IV of platelets. I look like I'm being drip fed a giant Capri sun. I look around the room for a moment; we're dressed in evening gowns and heels and look completely out of place.

"This is not how this night was supposed to go. I'm so sorry for ruining the formal for you," I tell her miserably. "I'm supposed to be getting felt up behind the gym right about now, not stuck in here with this." I grab my IV stand and rattle it for effect.

"I'd be happy to feel you up?" A deep voice echoes through the quiet room from behind us and we both spin around, wide-eyed, to see who's offering their groping services.

My eyes land on a tall, tanned dude with buzzed brown hair and a lip ring through his plump bottom lip. It takes my brain a few seconds to register that I've seen this person before. He's the hot-as-hell guy from Dr. Zahn's office. I lick my lips, hoping to add moisture to them; my mouth has suddenly turned into a desert. He's wearing a snug black T-shirt and tight black jeans, and... Shit, I'm staring.

Blair's shoulder nudges into mine subtly as she whispers under her breath, "I'd let him!"

I burst out laughing, like a moron, and feel my cheeks heat as the guy—Lucas, if I remember correctly, stands unmoving and staring right back at me. I'm greedily letting my eyes wander over him, comparing his physique and looks to Ethan before I register that he's holding his own IV stand. It's like a cold bucket of water over my head.

He's sick too.

"This is gonna sound weird, but I saw you come in, and I figured that life's too short right? I need to tell you that you're the hottest girl I've ever seen."

I look at Blair for confirmation that he did just say that, and her slack jaw endorses that it wasn't just in my head. "Wow, he's smooth." She laughs as he shoots me a brilliant white smile. Blair stands and announces that she needs coffee before smirking at me, and mouthing, "You're welcome," as she bails.

Leaving me here ... alone ... with Lucas... Hot, sexy, pierced, Lucas, who's smiling at me. And it's not one of those half-hearted smiles. It reaches his dark chocolate eyes and lights up his whole face.

Damn.

"I know you, right? You're the girl from my therapist's office," he states as he moves around to the front of me so I'm no longer twisting, and takes a seat.

"Yeah, I thought I recognized you. I'm Emily." I offer out my hand to shake. God only knows why. Who shakes hands these days? Ugh.

"Emily," he repeats as if he's trying the sound out to see if he likes it. He captures his lip ring between his teeth, and if he looked at my stats displayed on the monitor attached to my IV stand, he'd be able to see my heart rate increase because holy hell, *was that hot.*

"I'm Lucas," he says, stretching and taking my hand, giving it a little squeeze rather than a shake.

"I know." His eyes narrow in confusion. "Oh, I overheard your brother call you Lucas in Dr. Zahn's office," I clarify.

"And you remembered. Should I take that as a good sign?" His smile is still fixed in place and his eyes are boring into mine. I'm not sure how to respond to that, or even if I can get my brain and mouth to work together to organize a coherent thought and correctly-structured sentence. So I don't. Instead, I flash him a smile back.

I think it was the right answer.

ele

"Okay, Blair, I didn't just dream that up, right? Lucas was real, wasn't he?" I ask as Blair walks back into the common room thirty minutes later. My parents are hot on her heels.

"If by Lucas you mean that emo hottie with the piercing, then nope. He was very real." She smiles.

"Hmmm, would we call him emo? I'm not convinced. There was a distinct lack of guy-liner. Anyway, this shitty night just got a whole lot better because it means I didn't just imagine that kiss or his number in my cell," I say a little more enthusiastically than intended.

"You did not just kiss him!" she whisper-shouts as Mom and Dad rush up beside us to greet me, concern painted firmly across their faces. I answer her with a wiggled of my eyebrows, not wanting to say too much.

"Oh my god, you did!"

"Did what, honey?" Mom asks worriedly.

"Nothing," I reply softly, attempting to put her at ease.

"I'm so sorry, honey. This must have been a horrible night for you," Mom sighs.

"Actually, no." I smile genuinely. "It's been pretty awesome."

Chapter 12

THE FUNNY THING about kisses, especially a first kiss, is that they possess the power to render you stupid. One minute you're a perfectly normal girl, and the next minute your thoughts are scattered, breathing suddenly doesn't come so naturally anymore, and you can hear your own heartbeat thumping in your ears. Yet you embrace it, wandering blindly into the unknown with nothing but hopes.

Our kiss isn't even a timely affair. Nor is it a carnal, hunger-fueled, passionate collision of our mouths. It's a brief moment; a magical instance where time stands still and the earth stops spinning for the shortest of seconds. The only thing between us is the enchanting stir of anticipation as his face leans in close to mine. The weight of his lips is gone all too soon. Our eyes open as we pull apart and the air around us crackles. This one intensely perfect moment is over, and what should be the beginning, feels like the end. Realization sets in—where we are and what we're doing. And that old saying has never rung truer: *Never start what you can't finish.*

Maybe this is why we kiss and dream with our eyes

closed? The purest things in life are not meant to last. His kiss wasn't supposed to make me want another. He's not the object of my desire, I tell myself as I lie awake in my bed staring at his number in my cell. He's not Ethan, and I'm running out of time.

Sleep avoids me for the next few nights as I overanalyze the one quick kiss that I shared with Lucas, and then analyze my over-analysis. In all truth, I'm just one hot mess. It was supposed to be a chaste kiss goodbye; one of those, *It was great to meet you; let's get together sometime*, things.

Except it wasn't.

It was too slow and calculated.

He put his number into my cell and made me promise to call him. We'd only had a half hour of getting to know each other but it was easy, free-flowing conversation, streaked with little hints of flirting. *And I loved every second of it.*

I keep catching myself thinking, *why could it not be like this with Ethan?* Then I instantly feel like a bitch for comparing the two of them. Lucas was hardly ambiguous with his admission of liking me. You'd have to be a special brand of stupid to not notice how hot he his, and how genuine he comes across. *So why am I hung up on a boy who doesn't really even know I exist?* I could refocus my attention and have some fun while I have the opportunity, but even the thought sends an ache across my chest. I feel like I'm mourning the lost love of a boy who has never been mine.

I pull my pillow over my face and groan in frustration as I lie in bed with my journal open to my bucket list—

mocking me that I'm taking too long. *Stupid list!*

My cell vibrates on the nightstand and I reach over, pillow still in place, and fumble around, patting my hand along the cold wooden surface until it reaches its target. I peep from under the pillow and open up the text I just received. I bolt upright, the pillow dropping unceremoniously to the floor as I stare down at the message.

From: Lucas

A guy can only play it cool for so long before his ego takes a huge nose-dive. You didn't call? I feel like I've violated some unspoken guy code by contacting you first ;)

The message has my pulse racing and my fingers tingling as I wrack my brain, trying to think of an appropriate reply. I want it to be funny, but not at his expense; witty, but not sarcastic; flirty, without coming off like a giant whore.

One minute passes.

Two minutes.

Five minutes.

Seven minutes.

Screw it! Texting is overrated. I hit the call button and then instantly panic. *What if he picks up?* Or worse, *what if he doesn't?* I'll have to leave a voice message. "Shit," I curse and, of course, that's when the call connects.

"Wow, is that how you greet everyone you call?" I can hear the smile behind his words as my cheeks ignite. Thank goodness he can't see me.

"Sorry, no … I um, I wasn't expecting you to pick up so fast," I admit.

"I'm not going to lie. I thought you'd blown me off and ignored my text."

"You want the truth?" I ask, being careful to make my voice sound cheery rather than nervous as hell.

"Always."

"I've spent the last seven minutes trying to come up with a witty reply to impress you. Then I realized I'm not very witty, so I gave in and called."

A deep gruff laugh fills my room and I'm grinning from ear to ear that I prompted the sound.

"Well, just so you know, this is way better than a text. Unless you're calling to tell me to take a hike, in which case, you should have texted because it's gonna be all kinds of awkward when I start begging you to reconsider and let me take you out tomorrow night." There's a confidence to his voice that tells me he already knows my answer.

"Oh, okay … um, I guess we should embrace the awkwardness then," I deadpan.

The sharp intake of his breath is audible. "Really? Fuck, I thought you'd say yes. Okay, this *really* is awkward. So are you saying no to tomorrow? Or no to me in general?" he asks in a much flatter tone and I can't compress my giggle.

"I'm joking. Tomorrow is great."

"Wow, that was unnecessarily mean…" He trails off and I suddenly start to regret my retort. "I'm impressed," he continues. *Thank god.* I relax and lean back onto my bed as we discuss the logistics of our date tomorrow.

Holy crap.

I have a date.

ele

My home care nurse, Carla, visits with me while I'm in the midst of an internal meltdown about what to wear for this stupid date that I stupidly said yes to in a god damn stupid moment of weakness.

"Emily, are you sure you're feeling okay? You're looking really agitated," Carla remarks as she's making notes and taking down my weight. Apparently, the doctors need to keep a close eye on it. They don't want to over-dose me on the meds and accidentally kill me before the cancer gets a chance.

"I'm fine," I tell her, even though I know she'll call bullshit.

"Oh, fine … now there's a word I haven't heard used for everything but fine before!" she throws back at me. Carla is no-nonsense; she calls a spade a spade and isn't afraid to hurt your feelings like most other doctors and nurses who work in this particular field. We have a weird ten-second stand off where we each stare silently at the other before I crack.

"I have a date," I practically spit at her.

"And it's a bad thing because?" she draws out the word so it sounds like bee-cauzzzzz.

"I haven't told my parents or Blair, or anyone for that matter, except you."

She's looking at me confused, her eyebrows pull down to form a v and a frown appears on her normally cheery round face. Like she's not sure what she's missing.

"I don't want to feel judged. If I tell my folks, they'll be worried that I'm starting something up that will only upset me in the long run because I'll have to give it up. And let's face it, that won't be fair to anyone. And I haven't told Blair. She knows that I'm into someone else and I don't want her to think that I'm just using Lucas." I slump down next to her dramatically and wait for the magic advice to be doled out, eagerly wanting this guilty feeling that's manifesting inside of me to go away.

"Emily, I'm sure no one will judge you. If you want to go have fun with this Lucas boy, and he knows that's all it is, then go have it. You, of all people, should know that you only live once. If you're going to have regrets, let them be about what you have done, not about what you haven't. That's always been my motto."

"That's your professional opinion, is it?" I smirk.

"Heck no! My professional opinion is for you to go to your parents and Blair, and voice your concerns."

"Great, thanks," I huff, coming to a stand again as she gathers her paperwork, ready to leave.

"Let me know how your date goes," she says, stepping out the door and waving her goodbyes to my parents through the window. I ponder over her words as I walk back to my room. I don't want to tell anyone about Lucas, yet; I like that just for now, this is my own. Everything about my life for the last few years has been scrutinized. My body by doctors, my mind by therapists … the thought of actually having a secret causes a fizz of excitement in my stomach. If only I could ward off the surge of guilt that threatens to still it.

My mom and dad have a dinner planned with one of Dad's work colleagues and are leaving early to beat traffic and get to the restaurant on time. I mentally high-five the powers above. Not having to tell them I'm going on a date means I get to keep my clandestine meeting under wraps for now. At precisely six-thirty my parents leave, but not before instructing me to call if I need them.

In the last few days and weeks my body is beginning to slow down. Simple tasks are taking me longer to complete and I'm tired more. I put a pan of soup on the burner the day before yesterday because I was hungry, but I dozed off while I was sitting at the kitchen island waiting for it to heat and didn't wake until the smoke detectors started blaring. Mom came hurdling through to the kitchen in sheer panic noticed what I'd done and opened all the windows and doors to let out the thick smog that had formed. She looked depressed and defeated, although I could tell she was trying hard to conceal it. She's been reading through the pamphlets that Carla gave her the last time she visited. They're kind of a *'what to expect when you're expecting death'*. I've thought about reading them myself, but I decided I'd rather not know.

I'm slicking on another layer of mascara when the doorbell chimes. I look at my watch; he's ten minutes late. His tardiness makes me smile. Not because I have a weird fetish for being left waiting, but because I saw his car pull up fifteen minutes ago. I watched him from the bathroom window for a few minutes, wondering why he wasn't getting out the car. I figured he must be on a hands free call or something, so I went back to applying my make up. I'd be lying if I said that I wasn't starting to wonder if he'd had second thoughts and was going to drive away.

"You're late," I admonish in a playful tone as he stands at my doorway looking nothing short of edible.

"I know, and I'm sorry," he says as his eyes do an excruciatingly long scan of my whole body, setting my face ablaze. "You look beautiful," he whispers, leaning in and kissing my cheek in greeting. The gesture is friendly rather than flirtatious or sexual, and I feel instantly at ease. He moves back and bites down on the corner of his lip, dragging his teeth over the metal ring that adorns it. I'm not sure he's even aware that he's doing it, and I wonder if it's a nervous habit.

Either way, it's hot.

ele

If there is a prize for the best first date in the history of first dates, then I'm unequivocally certain that we've just taken the title. It wasn't the prerequisite dinner and movie, which I loved because really, who wants the awkward pre-dinner chatter that ends up feeling more like an interview? Just when you think you've been saved as the server brings your meals, you're faced with a new quandary: how the hell to not eat weird in front of each other as you struggle with the appropriate amount to devour. All the while trying to avoid,

a. Looking like a heifer.

b. Looking like a high-maintenance douche that won't eat anything other than salad because carbs are evil.

Then there's the completely unsociable forced silence a movie theater provides. Yeah, I'm beyond impressed that he thought outside the box for our date.

I climbed into his truck and he drove us straight to the grocery store, two minutes down the road. He pulled up, helped me out of the car, then retrieved forty dollars from his wallet and passed me a twenty-dollar bill. I'm not sure what the expression on my face looked like, but he seemed to find it amusing. He proceeded to tell me we were splitting up for fifteen minutes, and our challenge was to run through the store and pick out goodies for the other person. Anything goes, but we couldn't spend more than twenty dollars each.

I flew through the store like a crazy person, grabbing random items like chocolates, soda, and the ugliest six-dollar sleeveless T-shirt known to man, with a picture of a wolf on it. I stopped in the news aisle and grabbed the cheapest top shelf porn mag I could see. The elderly female cashier rang through my items, looking at me with complete disdain as she asked for my ID to approve the porn. I pulled it from my purse with a wide grin as she looked from me to the small rectangular card and back again. I think she may have even rubbed the tiny cross pendant hanging from her wrinkled neck at one point, no doubt praying silently for my depraved soul. I should have been embarrassed, uncomfortable at least, but I was having too much fun to care.

I exited the store out of breath and strode over to Lucas, swinging my loot as he rested against the hood of his dark blue truck watching me.

He looked at his watch. "You're cutting it close. You

only had a minute left before being disqualified," he warned, taking a step towards me and holding out his hand for my bag. He placed it in the truck beside his own and then opened my door for me. We drove across town with me badgering him about where he was taking me and why I couldn't look in the bag he'd bought for me. Patience has never been my strong point and he relished the fact that being kept in the dark was beginning to piss me off. He finally pulled up outside the entrance to the small children's play park, left deserted with the swings swaying eerily in the early evening Santa Ana breeze. I waited as he grabbed our bags, telling me we'd arrived.

"Time for part two," he mused and led me out into the dark playground.

"So, is this the part where you pull out cable ties and torture tools that you bought from the store and murder me?" I joked, though a small part of me was actually considering that might be the case. I didn't know anything about this guy really, only that the longer I was with him, the more he intrigued me.

He laughed awkwardly before telling me that there were plenty of things he'd like permission to do to me, but torture wasn't one of them. My head was screaming that this date was perhaps not the greatest idea. I didn't tell him that I was a ticking bomb and could detonate at any minute. The adrenaline surging through my system at his admission was messing with my body; I didn't know if I was panicked or turned on.

He did torture me in the park tonight. Not with cable ties and cruelty, but with kindness, fun, easy banter and comfortable silence. He tortured me with what I've been missing, and what I can't have. He'd spent his twenty dollars on a disposable picnic rug, strawberries and a bunch of brightly colored daisies. We lay in the park, staring at the stars and laughing about the fact that I was the only girl in his twenty years to have ever bought him porn, and how he would wear his T-shirt to our next date. I didn't tell him there likely wouldn't be one, just like I didn't mention my illness. He knows I'm sick, and I know he's sick, but we've made an unconscious decision to not bring it up yet.

It's been the best first date ever, and because of that, it's also the worst.

Chapter 13

I HAVEN'T TOLD a soul about my date.

I feel like I should be bragging about how awesome it was, but when Blair asked what I was up to last night, I shrugged and told her nothing special. The lie fell from my lips effortlessly. I don't like the deceitful feeling that slides over my skin, making it prickle, but I don't want the questions that will go with the revelation, either.

Mr. Wilde is lecturing the class on … Shit, I have no idea what, as I sit staring at my cell instead of the whiteboard. Blair's taking notes—she'll let me copy later.

From: Lucas
Is it too early to ask for date 2 already?

I type my reply, hit send and then wonder what the hell I was thinking.

To: Lucas
Yes! I had a great time, but there are things that you don't know about me, and another date will just

complicate things. Sorry, I really did have fun. X

Two seconds pass and my phone begins to vibrate. I quickly lift it from the desk, hoping Mr. Wilde doesn't hear it, and wait for it to stop as Blair mouths, "Who is it?" I shake my head and she narrows her eyes before turning back to the class. The vibrating stops and the screen lights up.

From: Lucas
Answer the phone, please.

My cell begins to vibrate again and I immediately cancel the call.

To: Lucas
I'm in class, can't answer.

From: Lucas
I do well with complicated. It's my specialty. You should give me a try. Call me when you get a chance?

I smile despite myself. My palms are sweaty and my stomach's in knots. He's persistent.

To: Lucas
I'll call you in an hour, when I'm on my lunch.

From: Lucas
I'll be waiting ;) X

I have an overwhelming feeling that I'm about to cry. I quickly grab my bag and my chair scrapes across the floor about as stealthily as a freight train. Figures. So much for sneaking out unnoticed. The sound alerts everyone and I look up to see Mr. Wilde, poised and ready to admonish the perpetrator. His glare meets mine, and recognition that it's me has his irritation waning. All my teachers are pretty tolerant of my coming and going as I please. I don't think any of them wants to be the one to reprimand me, since I'm here on borrowed time. His eyes soften and he lets my interruption slide as I motion to him that I need to leave. Blair whispers her concerns, asking if I'm okay, and I nod and tell her I'll be back before scurrying out of class.

The door closes with a dull thud and I lean against the lockers for a moment, trying to regroup. Ethan Jamison hurries past me and quickly opens his locker, grabbing a book and slamming the door closed again. I stare at his perfect profile as he shoves a hand through his dark hair: he's agitated. I take note of his long purposeful strides, and observe the sway of his tanned arms and the way his shirt pulls tightly over his back and shoulders. I catalogue all of this within three seconds, and he doesn't even notice me. He never has, and as I'm standing here now, I finally realize…

He never will.

The comprehension hits me with an unexpected force; it's the minuscule push needed to tilt my axis just a fragment too far. I barrel straight over the edge, the weight of my happily-never-after pulling me down, faster and faster as my tears come quickly. I run to the bathroom—the halls blurry through my watery vision—heave open the door and throw my bag across the floor, sending its contents rolling across the tiles. I hold my breath, then let out a low, strangled, toe-curling scream and kick the trashcan as hard as I can before sinking to the floor and giving my emotions free reign.

Emotional outbursts aren't normally my thing, especially in a public place, but the urge is just too great. I'm at school, for god's sake! I don't know what's come over me, but I do know that I hate it. I don't want to be weak, but I am. The exertion of crying is making me so short of breath that I'm panting. I used to be able to run ten kilometers without being this out of breath.

My head hurts. Come to think of it, my whole body is aching. I scan the floor, noticing my medication and cell underneath the basin where they'd rolled when I tossed my bag. I reach over and begin collecting all my crap from the grubby floor, cursing myself in the process and stop short on my hands and knees. I have a sudden moment of clarity, and the pitiful haze cloud I'm under begins to lift. *What the hell am I doing?*

I stand and splash cold water on my face, letting the coolness ease the heat behind my sore eyes. This isn't me. Emily Wilson wouldn't be caught dead crying in the school toilets.

elle

He answers on the second ring. "Geez, you're eager." The snap to my voice is unintended. There's a moment of silence that lasts a beat too long to be comfortable and I feel awful.

"How long do you have for lunch?" Lucas asks quietly and it does nothing to make me feel any better.

I sigh. I know I should stay at school, but I just can't. Today has lasted too long already. "I'm about to leave for the day now, so as long as I want, I guess," I'm careful to add a much lighter-hearted inflection to my tone of voice. I wait patiently for Lucas to answer. He's taking his time but I know he's still on the line because I can hear him breathing.

"I'm driving by your school now. Would you come and have lunch with me?" the hopefulness in his question is enough of a deterrent for me to not decline his offer.

"I'll be right back with your drinks and to take your order," a busty older lady announces, and I notice the wiry yellow hair shoved under her hat as she shows us to our seats. We're at Pete's Place, a small diner fifteen minutes from school. I like this place; it's retro. There's a huge Wurlitzer jukebox standing in the corner playing *Johnny B. Goode* while we decide what to eat. I couldn't face breakfast this morning, and I know it's not sensible to skip lunch, too, as it will only increase my lethargy, but I have zero appetite. I order food I don't want and hope I can stomach it when it's delivered.

"You think maybe we should address the giant pink ass elephant in the room and get it over and done with?" Lucas asks, looking at me so intently I feel his gaze on every part of my body. Not in some weird, sexual way, but more like if I asked him to close his big chocolate eyes right now and quizzed him on what I'm wearing, if I have freckles or what wrist I wear my bracelets on, he'd know. I have no doubt about it because when he looks at me, he pays attention.

I'm carefully folding my napkin into a tiny square, making it as small as I possibly can. "You mean, you want to know what it is about me that's complicated?" I ask, setting the napkin down and watching it spring open and unravel.

"I think I've narrowed it down to two possibilities," he says, watching carefully for my reaction. "You either have a boyfriend—"

I cut him off with my scoff and it's loud enough to have the couple sitting in the next booth looking over at us. "Trust me, Lucas, I most definitely do not have a boyfriend."

His shoulders drop ever so slightly in relief and it makes me smile. "Thank fuck," he sighs and the couple's heads turn back to us once more. I want to tell them it's rude to eavesdrop, but I suppose we are the ones dropping f-bombs. I swiftly wish he wasn't so relieved because the truth is so much harder to deal with than warding off a little male competition.

"Your second theory, Mr...." I have no clue what his surname is.

"Wade," he says, filling in the blank. He shuffles around in his seat and then looks up from his clasped hands. "I've come on too strong and scared you?" I can see the remorse in his features and my chest tightens.

"That's not it either, Lucas. Believe me, I wish it was."

"So, what is it then? Because I know this is full-on but I like you, Emily, and yesterday you did a pretty good job of acting like you maybe like me, too."

My pulse is racing. I can feel it as my mind frantically scrambles to figure out what to say to him. The truth really sucks sometimes.

"I'm sick, Lucas." *God I hate this.*

"I'm not sure if you've forgotten, Emily, but I met you in the oncology ward common room while we were both hooked up to IV's. I know you're sick. So, what is it?"

I chew on my cheek and then answer him. "A.L.L." He nods knowingly. Most people don't know what the acronym stands for and unaware it's cancer till you tell them it's Acute Lymphoblastic Leukemia.

"And?"

I know what he's asking and I almost choke as I answer, "Terminal."

Silence…

When he finally manages to look up from the table and acknowledge my response, his voice sounds flat and much quieter. "How long? I mean, do you know?"

I smile sadly because if I don't concentrate on trying to hold the fake grin in place, I'm scared the tears will come again. "Initially, six months. I'm on month four." I don't want a response, so I ask quickly, "What's your reason for hanging around in the oncology unit on a Saturday night, except to try pick up girls?"

A small chuckle escapes and he shifts, squaring his shoulders and focusing his full attention on me. "Tumor. Brain Stem Glioma. It's at the base of my brain," he tells me as I'm frozen in place. "It started off as a grade two, but because of where it is, surgery to remove it wasn't an option. Radiation therapy helped for a while, improved my chance of survival by slowing the tumor growth, but then it stopped working and it's on the increase again. I guess I'm what you could call fucked." He laughs, and there's actual humor to its lilt.

He's completely genuine, it's not a fake laugh that's laced with sarcasm, or one of those exasperated outbursts you do when the situation's too screwed to properly comprehend it. "I have a loaded gun lodged inside my head, and it's anyone's guess as to when it will fire." He's so matter-of-fact that it takes a minute for his words to sink in. "So, yeah, Emily, I understand complicated. But, you know what? Don't let something as minor as the fact that we're both on a timer bother you. Everyone is, when you think about it. No one lives forever. We're just a few rungs up on the ladder."

"Cheeseburger, no mayo," the waitress says in a bored, mechanical voice. The button on her shirt reads, 'Hi I'm Brenda, can I help?' I stare at it a moment as Lucas claims the food.

"Hawaiian burger," she monotones and I place my hand up. I don't trust my voice. My eyes fix on Lucas's and I want to say something, anything, but there's nothing there. No words. He picks up the ketchup bottle and starts squeezing it over his fries and I watch him act like we've not just discovered that we're both well and truly screwed.

I don't want to fucking die, and now my heart hurts because I don't want Lucas to die, either.

14

September 17th, 2013
(*3 Months)

Dear Diary…

 I think I've exhausted every article I could find on the Internet about Brain Stem Glioma. It's funny how I won't type ALL in to the search bar. I've been taught that the Internet is not a reliable source of medical information. My doctors, parents, even Blair warned me to stay away from researching it online. Just stick to the information that the hospital provides, they all agreed. I'm assuming this is the norm for most cancer sufferers; they're warned away from the web and the countless sites offering false hope in the form of untested, highly expensive miracle drugs. I know all this, but despite it, as soon as Lucas gave me his diagnosis, I jumped online at the very first opportunity.

 I read through a comment thread in one forum that's had me in tears for two hours straight. Some of the entries were from the patients themselves; others by family and loved ones. I can't help wonder if anyone I know has done a similar thing and asked questions about what to expect and how to cope when I'm gone. The thought turns my stomach.

I don't know what it is I'm looking for, reading all these articles. Maybe I'm just grasping at straws and searching for a miracle.

I spent most of the day with Lucas before my little cyber binge. We talked for hours about everything and nothing. I told him about my list. Well, actually, I showed him the copy I have on my cell. He's the first and only person that knows of its existence. His eyebrows almost shot through the roof when he saw the virginity check box, which then prompted a bunch of questions. I told him all about Ethan and the fact that he doesn't seem to know I exist. I think his response was, "If the guy hasn't noticed you, Emily, then he's clearly got some heavy stuff that's distracting him. And if not, he's clearly gay, which means you should change the name on your list and refocus your attention on me." I laughed, but I'm not convinced that he wasn't being serious.

He couldn't understand that I'd never slept beneath the stars; I explained that I'd been camping before, but never just slept under the night sky. He insisted that he's picking me up tomorrow night and taking me to do just that. I told him I'd think about it. I want to, but I'm not sure that I dare. Sharing that with him might be too intimate. I don't know.

I guess he just scares me because he makes me hope, and there's no room for that in the time I have left. I'm not scheduled for a happy ever after, and I'd finally put myself at peace with that. But now here he comes along, like Prince Charming's sexy pierced brother, and something's shifting.

I'm scared.

ele

"The girls are here!" Mom shouts, seconds before I can hear Brie's voice operating at a mile a minute. I'm on my bed, too tired to get up and greet them, but I know they'll soon make their way to me. Blair is the first to pop her head around my door.

"Hey, Em, room for a small one?" she asks, proceeding to climb up onto my bed and lie beside me on her back.

"No," I deadpan jokingly and she twists her head to look at me in mock offense.

"Tough, I'm not budging. I'm too comfy."

I laugh as she sticks her tongue out at me like a bratty kid, and Casey and Brie barrel into the room, jumping up on my bed, too.

"Oh my gosh, you guys," Casey begins with the widest grin I've ever seen her sport. "Brie is about to make your day. Listen to this!"

"Gee, thanks … friend," Brie groans out unenthusiastically, blowing a strand of her long blonde hair out of her face.

I look at Blair for some sort of clue as to what's going on but she looks as lost as me. "What's happened?" I ask, sitting up and crossing my legs, poised for gossip.

"You know the—"

"Um, excuse me, Casey! I thought you wanted me to tell them," Brie says, giving her a look that clearly means 'shut the hell up'. Casey smirks, and Brie rolls her eyes.

"You know the barista guy from The Grind who I had a date with?" Blair and I nod while Casey's grin stretches even wider. She obviously knows this story.

"The one you won't talk about to anyone?" I confirm and her head drops a fraction.

"That's the one," she says flatly. "Well, I'm only telling you this now because I got drunk at one of TJ Conner's parties this past weekend, and apparently told everyone on the volleyball team, so I guess you'll hear a blown-up version of it at school this week. I met Marcus, you know the Barista Babe, the next day at The Grind like he told me to."

"Um, yeah, after telling all the girls on the cheer squad she was dating him already, before she even showed up to their first date!" Casey squeals and I swear I see murder flash over Brie's face.

"Oh my gosh, Case, let me finish! So yeah, I went to meet him after telling the team I was already dating him because I thought it was a given. Anyway, I show up and he's sitting at a table with this insanely good-looking guy. Like seriously, the two of them looked like a pair of Abercrombie models. I walk over and Marcus stands to greet me, gives me a kiss on both cheeks, you know, like they do in Europe, and he introduces his friend, Paulo. Paulo does the whole two kisses thing and motions for me to sit down and join them. At this point, I'm thinking Paulo will be leaving soon and Marcus and I can get to the date part. Well, that didn't happen."

Casey is giggling like a toddler beside us and I'm wondering where the hell the story's going.

"It turns out that Paulo is Marcus's boyfriend … of three years! And the reason he didn't tell me he was gay when I was asking him out was because I was so brazen and overconfident in front of you guys that he didn't want to embarrass me any more than I already was. You know, since I'd taken the coffee bath, and all."

Blair and I look at each other, then at Brie, who's shaking her head, clearly hating the fact that she's had to fess up to this, and then at Casey, who looks like the weird smiley cat from *Alice in Wonderland*. We all burst out laughing as Brie sits stoic, fighting the smile I can see making the corners of her mouth twitch.

"That *was* kind of nice of him," Blair says. "It *would* have been more embarrassing if he'd done it in the coffee shop in front of us. At least he was considerate."

"No, Blair, what's embarrassing is that I've told half the school I'm dating a guy who's in a full-time committed relationship with another guy! I'm going to sound like such a desperate psycho when everyone finds out. Ugh!"

"Dude, everyone thinks that anyway!" Casey says in a mock comforting tone as she pats her on the shoulder. Brie begins to laugh with us because, well, it's kind of true.

ele

By the time the girls leave I'm in a great mood. No doubt some of that is because I'm medicated off my ass, but I'm feeling pretty good—light, even—so I text Lucas and tell him I'm on for crossing off a check box, and to pick me up after dinner tomorrow. His reply is almost instant and has me giggling like a moron.

From: Lucas

This will technically be our second date, and you're willing to sleep with me. That makes me question your morals! Good thing you're cute and I don't have any! ;) X

A swarm of butterflies feel like they've taken flight in my stomach, and I'm momentarily taken aback. The only person I can ever remember having butterflies over is Ethan. It's a bittersweet feeling.

I walk down to the family room on shaky legs; the medication I'm on makes me forget that my body isn't working the way it always has. It's a sucky reminder, but I'm not dwelling on it. What's the point?

My parents are watching a movie as I slip quietly in to the room. I need to take a deep breath to steady my nerves.

"Hey, poppet, what's up?" Dad asks. He shifts so that Mom can sit up; her head was resting in his lap while watching the film.

"I have a question, and you're probably not going to like it, but I'm asking out of respect and I hope you'll agree to it out of respect."

They look at each other, seemingly intrigued and worried by my odd request. "Okay, shoot. What is it?" Dad asks, rubbing his chin and pinching his bottom lip.

"I want to go camping tomorrow with a guy I met at

the hospital, Lucas. Before you jump to anything, we're just friends. He's really sweet and we're both in the same boat. He's sick, too. I know you haven't met him, but I know you'd like him. Please?"

It takes forty-five minutes of tears and explaining why I want to do this one thing before I die for them to relent. Not because they don't trust me, or my judgment of Lucas, but because I'm supposedly too sick to be outside all night. It's kind of ironic, really; I laugh and ask them what's the worst that can happen. It kills me? They don't laugh back, but they do finally agree.

We spend the rest of the evening huddled on the couch watching some boring film Dad chose. Mom has to get me blankets because my legs, feet and hands are always cold now. Dad makes me promise to take my comforter, sleeping bag and extra blankets tomorrow. I probably won't last the whole night outside, but I love that they're willing to let me try.

ele

"So, you only told your folks about me last night, and they're okay with me bringing you here?" Lucas asks as he pulls his truck into the field behind his parents' farmhouse.

We bump along the dirt road until we enter a clearing and he parks. We're going to be sleeping in the back of his truck tonight. He's put a mattress on the flatbed to make it as comfy as possible, and he looks to have enough blankets stacked in the back to construct the world's biggest blanket fort. We're on his property as per the instructions of his dad; he wanted us close enough to the house so that we can bail if we need to for any reason.

"I wouldn't really say that they're okay. More like they're allowing it under protest. I can't really blame them for not wanting me to do this. I'm in some random field with a boy I know very little about. By anyone's standards, a sleepover for a second date is a little strange. Plus, when we run out of things to talk about in an hour, this is going to seem like such a bad idea." I give my mini speech light-heartedly, but I am a tad worried that the conversation is going to dry up because it's kind of inevitable, and things will get awkward. I've never shared a bed with a guy be-fore, or spent an entire night alone with one, for that mat-ter. I think my nerves are justified.

"You know, I could just go for the accidental boob graze now and get it out of the way. Then we can make out till our lips are numb and fall asleep from the sheer ex-haustion of fighting to keep our clothes on, when what we really want to do is rip each other's off. And at least this way, you don't have to panic about the conversation?" He's completely straight faced and I feel goose bumps race over my body.

I let out a nervous ... well, I don't know what to clas-sify it as ... squeak, maybe? My toes curl in my sneakers and I begin to fidget with the hem of my sweater.

"I'm joking, Emily." He nudges me and it does noth-ing but raise my pulse further. "If you feel uncomfortable at any point, just tell me and I'll drive you home. You're not obligated to be here or spend time with me. I don't want to make you feel awkward. I just wanted to help you cross off some of those points on your list."

There's a sincerity to Lucas that is so endearing to

me. I only wish I could have met him sooner. His chocolate eyes are mesmerizing as they stare into mine and I feel like we're having a moment. I watch as he drags his teeth over the silver ring in his bottom lip and it curls when he notices I'm focused on it.

"Do you have any more piercings?" I ask, not even meaning to. It was the first thing that popped into my head and now I'm having a hard time dragging my attention away from his mouth.

"No, just this one. What about you?" Ugh, well that just put a damper on the nipple-piercing images flashing through my mind.

"My ears are pierced, but that's it. I have a tattoo, though. Do you have any?" He looks like the type of guy who would have a tattoo. Maybe some sort of tribal art over his shoulders and down his back. *Yum.*

"You have a tattoo? Nah, I'm gonna call bullshit. You look far too straight-laced. And yeah, I have one I got about two years ago,"

"I do too have a tattoo. I'll make you a deal. You show me yours and I'll show you mine."

"Why do I feel like I'm at a weird show-and-tell all of a sudden?" He chuckles before pulling his shirt up to uncover his smooth tanned skin. As I suspected, there's literally not an ounce of fat on him. My eyes roam the dips and piques of his abs all the way up to the tattoo above his heart. It's in thin black script, and I move closer so I can read it.

Work for a cause, not for applause. Live life to express, not to impress. Don't strive to make your pres-

ence noticed, just make your absence felt.

"Nice." I nod in approval of not just the words, but everything else I'm looking at.

He pulls his shirt back into place and gives me a wicked smile. "I do believe it's your turn now." He wiggles his eyebrows playfully and rubs his hands together as he shifts, pretending to make himself comfy. I wrack my brain, trying to remember what bra I'm wearing, but I draw a blank. I just hope to hell that I'm not wearing my favorite, which used to be white, but now is a depressing shade of grey. It probably should be gracing the bottom of a trashcan but I keep it because it's just so damn comfy.

I pull the side of my sweater up to just below the purple lace of one of my nicer bras, displaying the tree tattoo.

"It's supposed to represent the circle of life. You know, how it goes on," I offer, unexpectedly feeling like I need to justify it.

"It's nice." He coughs, clearing his throat, and repeats it again with a clear, less gruff tone.

"Thanks." *Okay, this just got weird.*

"This is weird, isn't it?"

"Yes! Oh my god, I was just thinking that."

"You know, it might help if you pull your sweater back down." He smirks and I feel my blush spread like a forest fire across my chest and up my neck.

Why the fuck am I still holding my top up? Idiot. I pull it down, but can't hold a straight face, and apparently, neither can Lucas.

Chapter 15

"ARE YOU COLD?" His breath fans across my face. He's leaning in close, resting on one of his elbows.

I'm staring at the millions of stars that I feel like have come out just for me tonight. I stay fixed in place, fascinated by the stillness above me. "A little, I suppose. Not too bad."

"Here."

He drags over another blanket and cocoons me in it. I'm fighting the urge to smile. He's attentive and sweet; as attracted as I am to him physically, he's winning me over mentally, too.

"What?"

"What?"

"You're pulling a strange face. Do you want to head back inside?"

"No!" I don't mean to shout it so loud, but without any other noise to compete with, it tears through the atmosphere like a sonic boom.

"Wow, chill. I was just checking," he says as he buries himself down into the covers and mirrors my position, facing the heavens. It's quiet for a few beats before I hear him sigh. I'm pretty sure he's working up to saying something.

"Are you scared?"

I know what he's asking as I close my eyes and really think about my answer.

"Yes. Not of the actual dying part. I know that's not going to be nice, don't get me wrong, but that's not what's been keeping me up at night. I'm scared of that being it. What if there's no heaven? Or rebirth? It can't be just fade to black and then that's it, can it?"

"I don't think so. I mean, our bodies are going to stop working and shut down, but what happens to our souls? There's no physical part of us that *is* our soul, so there must be somewhere they go."

"I like the thought of that," I murmur.

It's peaceful for a long time after that. Nothing interrupts the tranquility until his hand moves slowly under our blankets, in search of mine. He laces our fingers together and it's possibly the simplest and most intimate moment I've ever shared. I never want it to end. I can feel the heat of his thumb rubbing along the top of my own as I close my eyes tight, but it's too late. The cool night air freezes the damp trail the traitorous lone tear leaves down the side of my face. If he notices, he doesn't say anything, and it makes me like him that much more.

"I can't get your list out of my mind." It's barely audible, like he's not sure whether it's okay to be mentioning it or not.

"Why?"

It's not like it has anything that radical on it, so I'm

not sure what it is that's playing on his concentration. He turns so he's facing me and drops my hand. I'm disappointed by the loss, even though I know I shouldn't be. I turn so I can look at him, too. I feel self-conscious, knowing that he's staring at me.

"You've never been in love," he states. His words sit heavily on my chest.

I look down from his eyes; they look sorry, and I'm not sure if it makes me feel embarrassed or pitiful, but either way, I suddenly feel childish. "I've been in lust," I huff out defensively. "But no, you're right. I've never been in love. That doesn't mean I haven't known love, though," I offer. "I love my family, Blair, my friends … and I know they all love me."

"It's not the same, though," he whispers and a wave of grief races down my spine. "I don't want you to die not knowing what it's like." His words are like a thousand tiny needles pricking at my skin.

"I don't either." It's one of my biggest fears. My eyes begin to well, and the back of my throat abruptly begins to tighten and hurt from holding back a sob fighting to escape.

"So let me show you?" I feel a tear leak as I narrow my eyes in confusion.

"What?"

"Let me show you. Let me make you fall in love with me."

My tears hit full force and I'm not sure if I'll be able to make them stop. He crushes my body against his in a tight embrace and I cry a silent torrent of tears into his shirt while he holds me wordlessly.

I've exhausted myself by the time I pull away. He looks down at me and I must look awful, but he's considering me like I look anything but. His beautiful dark eyes are fixed on my own, and he's breathing deeply. The fabric of his shirt has darkened where my tears have soaked through and it jolts my awareness of what's just happened.

"I'm sorry, I don't even know where that came from." I feel like I need to apologize for having a meltdown, but stop when he shakes his head vehemently.

"Don't. You've nothing to be sorry for. I didn't mean to upset you. Shit, this played out so much better in my head. Look, Emily, I'm attracted to you, you must know that, and not just a little bit. You're amazing, and if things were different, I'd take my time. I'd pursue you the way you deserve. I'd buy you flowers and bug you to date me. I'd spend time winning over your folks, and wearing you down until you had no other option but to fall for me. That's not what's in our cards, though, and I know it's rushed, and I get it if you want me to back the fuck off. But I know I could love you so damn easily, Emily. It would be no effort at all. I want … fuck, I *need* you to let me try and win your heart because I've never met anyone who deserves to know what love is more than you."

The butterflies are back, but I think they've invited a swarm of lightning bugs to join them. My insides feel alive with an electric current and I have absolutely no idea what to say. He's watching me carefully, patiently waiting for me to do or say something, but what?

I lean forward, never breaking eye contact. This is the single most nervous I've ever felt, but it's not a bad feeling. Just … terrifying. His eyes widen slightly as I move closer and closer. His tongue darts out, quickly wetting his lips, and my nose brushes against his. The contact ignites a blaze deep inside of me and for the first time in weeks, I'm actually too warm. My mouth lands slowly on top of his. He drags in an unsteady breath, and then begins moving his hands slowly up the back of my neck and cradles my head as he pulls me tighter to him. I've kissed a few guys before, but never like this, and I'm quickly realizing how amateur I must feel to him in contrast to how skilled, and frankly, fucking amazing he feels to me.

There's a groan and I don't know if it's his or mine, but I feel him smile through the kiss before his tongue invades my mouth. The coolness of his lip ring fights with the heat of his mouth and every coherent thought I have in my head begins to escape. We kiss until we're both completely breathless, which happens way too fast for my liking. He pulls back and watches my reaction as our chests heave and our breathing starts to even out.

"Is that a yes?" He smiles.

I feel completely out of my depth, but I'm more sure about this than I've been about anything else in a long time. "If you think you can." I smile coyly.

"Trust me, I *know* I can." He flips me and pulls my back flush against his chest, snaking his arm gently over my stomach.

And that's how we stay.

There's no more kissing, no awkwardness or silence that we feel the need to fill. We talk for hours under the stars until I finally fall asleep. And when I wake, I send a silent prayer of thanks that this wasn't just a dream.

elle

Lucas drops me home and I make it three feet into the house before Mom and Dad pounce on me. I tell them I had a nice evening, leaving out the part where the mysterious boy I barely know made it his mission to get me to fall in love with him. I'm sure they know something has happened because I can't keep the silly grin off my face. Dad doesn't know whether to smile or scowl at me, so I decide to square things up for him.

"Just so you guys know, when I left the house last night I was a virgin."

Mom almost drops her coffee and Dad's face is noticeably a few shades paler.

"I'm still one now, so you can relax."

And with that I grin and head to my room. I can't hear them talking, I think I've rendered them speechless with my little outburst. I know it will ease their minds, though. *When they can think straight again.*

I take a two-hour bath to try and warm my body back up. I'm stiff from sleeping outside, even though Lucas's mattress was pretty soft. I soak in the water until it makes my body wrinkle and then pull myself from the soothing hot water and wrap myself in my robe.

Blair is sitting on my bed when I walk into my room, and I let out a startled shriek. "Jesus, you scared the life out of me!" I laugh.

"Your mom said it was fine to come wait in here. Sorry, I should have called out so you knew I was in here."

"It's fine. My poor weak heart almost jumped out of my mouth though. So, whatcha up to?"

"Not much." She shrugs. "I feel like I haven't seen you in ages, even though I see you almost every day. I don't know … I'm being stupid, I guess. I watched a film last night about a girl who was dying and her sister could maybe help her, but she didn't want to put her through it. Honestly, it was the dumbest thing I've ever done. I don't know what possessed me, but I don't think I've stopped crying for more than five minutes since." Her eyes fill with tears as she's telling me this. It's so out of character for Blair; she's one of the strongest people I know. I sit next to her and reach for her hand.

"I'm not ready for this, Em. It's not fair, and I know I shouldn't be saying this to you, of all people. But it's gotten to the point where I have to say it. I love you, and I'm not ready. I wish I could do something. If I could give you my bone marrow or anything else that might give you more time, I would. I wouldn't need to think twice about it; I'd do it in an instant."

"I know, Blair, I love you too. And you know what?"

"What?" she asks shakily.

"I'm banning you from any and all cancer-related films from this point forward. You're the ugliest crier I've ever met." She lets out a snort and there's snot and tears bubbling from her nose.

"Oh my god, gross!" I laugh and nudge her shoulder.

"You shouldn't make me laugh while I cry. You know it's never going to end well." She walks over to my nightstand and grabs a tissue.

"Seriously, you okay now? Feel better for getting that off your chest?"

"The snot or the meltdown?"

"Eww. Both, I guess." I shrug.

"Yep, I swear I won't do that again. Damn you, Jodi Picoult!"

My phone beeps on my bed and I reach over, snatching it up before Blair sees Lucas's name flash on the screen. I open up the message and wince at the size; it's like a college dissertation.

From: Lucas
Hey! So, phase one. I saw this online, and it's got to be worth a shot, right? Apparently, this study by a psychologist named Arthur Aron has been proven to make you fall in love by answering 36 questions. Grab some padding, sweetheart, because I'm gonna make you fall hard! Oh, and sorry, I know there's a shit load of them. Also, we need to stare at each other for a full 4 minutes silently at the end. Personally, I think we should do this ASAP. Just saying! ;)

I click on the file that's attached to his message and begin to read.

1. Given the choice of anyone in the world, whom would you want as a dinner guest? *Hint, me!*

2. Would you like to be famous? In what way?

3. Before making a telephone call, do you ever rehearse what you are going to say? Why?

4. What would constitute a "perfect" day for you?

5. When did you last sing to yourself? To someone else?

6. If you were able to live to the age of 90 and retain

either the mind or body of a 30-year-old for the last 60 years of your life, which would you want?

7. Do you have a secret hunch about how you will die? ***I think we can skip this one! :/***

8. Name three things you and your partner appear to have in common.

9. For what in your life do you feel most grateful? ***Pay-per-view porn … Jokes!***

10. If you could change anything about the way you were raised, what would it be?

11. Take four minutes and tell your partner your life story in as much detail as possible.

12. If you could wake up tomorrow having gained any one quality or ability, what would it be?

13. If a crystal ball could tell you the truth about yourself, your life, the future or anything else, what would you want to know?

14. Is there something that you've dreamed of doing for a long time? Why haven't you done it?

15. What is the greatest accomplishment of your life?

16. What do you value most in a friendship?

17. What is your most treasured memory?

18. What is your most terrible memory?

19. If you knew that in one year you would die suddenly, would you change anything about the way you are now living? Why? ***I think we can skip this one too … Sorry!***

20. What does friendship mean to you?

21. What roles do love and affection play in your life?

22. Alternate sharing something you consider a positive characteristic of your partner. Share a total of five

items.

23. How close and warm is your family? Do you feel your childhood was happier than most other people's?

24. How do you feel about your relationship with your mother?

25. Make three true "we" statements each. For instance, "We are both in this room feeling ..."

26. Complete this sentence: I wish I had someone with whom I could share ... *My smoking hot body, and I wish his name were Lucas Wade ;)*

27. If you were going to become a close friend with your partner, please share what would be important for him or her to know.

28. Tell your partner what you like about them; be very honest this time, saying things that you might not say to someone you've just met.

29. Share with your partner an embarrassing moment in your life... *Apart from being sent a list of questions stolen from the Internet to make you fall in love with some dumbass that won't leave you alone!*

30. When did you last cry in front of another person? By yourself?

31. Tell your partner something that you like about them already.

32. What, if anything, is too serious to be joked about?

33. If you were to die this evening with no opportunity to communicate with anyone, what would you most regret not having told someone? Why haven't you told them yet?

34. Your house, containing everything you own,

catches fire. After saving your loved ones and pets, you have time to safely make a final dash to save any one item. What would it be? Why?

35. Of all the people in your family, whose death would you find most disturbing? Why?

36. Share a personal problem and ask your partner's advice on how he or she might handle it. Also, ask your partner to reflect back to you how you seem to be feeling about the problem you have chosen.

I'm giving you the heads up on these questions. Be ready to answer them tomorrow! I'm picking you up for date number three. That's a reasonable amount of dates before falling in love right? ;) X

I've spent so long reading the text that when I look up I realize I've forgotten Blair's here. She's watching me intently and I feel like I've just been caught doing something really underhanded.

"What's going on?" she asks, peering over my shoulder.

I clear the screen. "Nothing, just Lucas, texting me." I smile.

"Lucas? Wait … Emo Hottie from the hospital Lucas?

I laugh. I'm not sure if Blair even understands what an emo is. "Dude, he's not emo, but yeah, that Lucas."

"Whatever, you know who I meant. So, how long has he been texting you?" She wiggles her eyebrows and I roll my eyes in response.

"Not long, relax. Anyway what's new with you? Anything new to report? Brie and Casey haven't done anything newsworthy I need to know about?" I'm changing the subject and by the look she's shooting me, she knows exactly what I'm doing but she lets me anyway. She's kind of awesome like that.

Chapter 16

October 1ˢᵗ, 2013
(*2 Months)

Dear Diary

It's been two weeks since Lucas and I did the Dr. Aron love questions. I'm not entirely sure they've worked. I don't know if I'm in love with him just yet, but I *am* loving how hard he's trying. I've picked up a chest infection, so I'm pretty much housebound at the moment. His texts are the only thing keeping me sane between Blair and Nurse Carla's ever-increasing visits. I think she kind of blew us all away when she visited yesterday. She asked that my parents and I sit in the family room, because she had some questions for us. We got comfy on the sofa—I was sitting between Mom and Dad—and then, BAM!

She hit us with the 'Where do you want to die, Emily?' question. I'm pretty sure a little piece of all of us died right there and then. I like Carla, she's truly a lovely woman, but as she launched into her speech about how many people choose to die at home, where they feel safe and comfortable, she dropped a few notches on my favorite persons list, and I kind of wanted to punch her in the throat. I'm not normally a person who has violent thoughts, but I could have used a little more warning before springing that particular question on me. If I listened hard enough, I bet I'd have heard my parents' hearts shatter.

"Your surroundings would be familiar and you can be in the presence of friends and family," Carla continued and I think I just shut down. "The hospice doctors and nurses will work with other professionals in the community to care for you at home if that is what you want."

I nodded and then retreated back to my room. I'm not sure there was any way the day could have been rescued from the depths of how much it sucked to have to discuss that type of thing. It took a long time to fall asleep last night. I'm becoming more and more restless and this stupid chest infection has me wheezing like I smoke sixty a day.

I read the leaflets that Carla left with Mom this morning. They were more reassuring than I thought they'd be. One went into detail about how my care team can ensure my parents will not be alone in caring for me—they'll have help and support. It put my mind at rest. It's something that's been nagging at me, and I didn't know how to broach the subject. I know caring for someone at home can be emotionally and physically draining. I've seen the effects first-hand with some of the parents from the hospital. I don't want to put *that* on my parents, but I want to be here in our home with them when it's time.

I've written them a letter for when I pass. It's the

worst pain I've ever felt, knowing that I'm going to leave them. I hate this feeling.

I don't want to end this entry on a bad note, so I'm going to share the highlight of my day so far. It was a text message from Lucas, and it made me laugh when I thought I had nothing else to laugh about.

From: Lucas

Hey, good looking. I bought a chick magazine to-day at the grocery store. This is what YOU'VE reduced me to. The front cover said this month's issue features an article on how to fall in love. So I bought it, along with a car magazine to balance out the fact that I seem to have misplaced my nuts. I've saved it for you, btw ;) I read it as soon as I got home. Basically it was an article on how you should love yourself before you can expect anyone to love you in return. So that's what I did. I spent an hour 'loving myself' (with the help of the magazine you bought for me on our first date). Also, chick magazines are pretty filthy. Girls talk about some weird shit. Anyway, just thought you should know that I do love myself, quite frequently. Feel free to fall in love with me too anytime soon :D X

What's not to love, right?

Blair visits every day without fail now. I haven't made it to school in a while and since I've been cooped up at home, I've discovered something I thought was lost.

Hope.

When I first found out that I was dying, I was caught up in the huge amount of averages and statistics that doctors offered me about how quickly my cancer was likely to progress and how long I had left to live. I thought I wanted to know, but as soon as the figures were given to me, I wanted to hand them back and reclaim my blissful ignorance. Yes, thinking about it now, it's helpful to know those things, but they didn't exactly provide me with any type of comfort. In fact, it was the opposite. Once I knew my averages, I was scared to death. Certain that there was no hope for me, the doctors had done all they could do, science had failed, and that was that.

Over the past few weeks, I've begun to find hope in the future. I'm not talking months or even weeks into the future, but days … tomorrows. Little things that I've unknowingly taken for granted. Visits from Blair, Casey and Brie, phone calls, texts and dates with Lucas. I look forward to them, so they're a kind of hope, right? Bottom line: they're a reason to live, and I should look for those reasons, that hope, despite having only one month, one year or one decade left to live.

ele

I'm writing Blair's letter. I keep reading it back and wondering if I should try and make it sound happier. I don't want it to upset her.

Blair,

   If you're reading this then I've obviously croaked it. Lol! I know it's not funny but I kinda have to make a joke of it so that what I'm writing doesn't feel so real, you know? I'm writing this letter to you after just finishing the one I've written for my parents. I need to lighten the mood, so I'm gonna confess something. I can say it now because I'm not here anymore and there'll be no retaliation. It's a cheap trick, but you know you love me.

   Last year when Corey Spencer asked you out, and then cancelled at the last minute, I may or may not have accidentally told him that you used to write Mrs. Blair Spencer and practice your signature at the back of your journal.

   And I may have also told him that you had your kids' names picked out already. I know, I know, I totally freaked him out! I thought he'd laugh and tease you about it on your date, but I guess he kinda thought you were a bunny boiler and bailed. Sorry!!!

   Okay, so now that I have that off my chest, I need you to do something for me and you can't say no because it's a dying girl's wish! Yeah, I know, I played the dying BFF card. But please, just think about it.

   I want to ask her to finish doing all of the things on my list. But how would I even word something like that? And honestly, why would anyone do it? It's not like I'll ever know. I can't help thinking that I'm not going to finish the list in my current state of health, but I don't want to fail. If I can't complete it, she's the only person on the entire planet I would want to do it for me. Maybe I should ask her about this in person? It seemed like a good idea, doing it via letter, but now, not so much. I need to put more thought into it.

I need more time.

The doorbell chimes and I assume it's going to be Blair who walks into the kitchen, but it's not. Instead, Lucas is standing in a pair of faded gray jeans and a plain white T-shirt. Damn, he looks hot.

"Hey, beautiful, how are you?" he asks, placing a quick kiss on my cheek and sitting across the breakfast bar from me.

"I'm good. What are you doing here?" I don't mean for it to come out like he's not welcome, but I see a flash of hurt pass over his face and it makes my chest ache. "That came out wrong. I'm glad you're here," I add.

"Thanks. I called your cell and there was no answer. I just wanted to check in on my favorite girl." He stares at me, holding my gaze, and there's something off about it.

"Um, what's with the staring?"

His head doesn't move and his eyes never stray from mine as he answers. "My dad said that to fall in love, a woman has really got to see you, so I figured I'd come and stare at you until you gave in and admitted your affections for me. Why, am I creeping you out?" he asks playfully.

Instantly, the heavy mood I was in lightens. "You're one strange boy, Lucas Wade."

"Sweetheart, I'm no boy, I can assure you of that," he says with a cocky grin that has me laughing my ass off.

"You know, I thought you'd have given up on me by now."

"Yeah, well, I thought we'd be on our honeymoon after our shotgun Vegas wedding by now. Guess we both thought wrong." He's sporting one of his wide gorgeous smiles. I pull my cream sweater tightly around me as a shiver runs down my back. I'm wearing it over a vest and yoga pants, but despite the unseasonably warm weather, I'm still cold.

"Here," he says, walking around the counter, "let me warm you up." He encloses me in a circle, pulling me into his chest, and I sigh with the comfort his arms bring. He should sell hugs. He'd be a billionaire in no time. His chin rests on my head and then his arm reaches out to the counter, moving my draft of Blair's letter and my list sitting under it. I stiffen and so does he. The thought of him reading things I've written about another guy feels wrong now that I've spent so much time with him. I feel a weird sense of guilt, even though I've already told him about Ethan.

"You still hung up on this Ethan guy?" he says in a voice so quiet it's barely audible. For a moment, I don't know what to answer. I've been borderline infatuated with the guy for so long now that it's almost become second nature to be interested in anything about him. Something's shifted in me these past few weeks, though. I'm not so interested in Ethan anymore.

I've spaced out in my moment of enlightenment and have not replied to Lucas's question. I can feel his body sag as he moves back to look at me.

"I can't compete, can I? You've already given your heart away."

Silence stretches between us and my mind is running through a million responses of how to explain that he's wrong, but the signals just don't seem to be filtering down to my mouth so I can actually speak them.

"Silence…not a good sign." His head drops and when he lifts it to look at me seconds later, there's so much hurt in his eyes. Knowing I've caused it feels like a sucker punch.

"I know that this Ethan guy has your heart, Emily, but I want you to know that you have mine. You've had it from the second you walked into the hospital that day in your blue dress." His lips find mine for the lightest of kisses and before I can reach up to hold him in place, they're gone.

"I love you, Em. I want you to know that. And I don't mean like a friend. I'm *in* love with you, and this aching inside my chest … I want you to know that I wouldn't change it, not for a second."

I blink away my tears in time to see him make his way to the door and my throat closes up. I want to shout for him to wait but I can't. He disappears out of sight and it takes a few seconds before my paralysis lets go and I realize what's just happened. This conversation got way out of hand, far too fast. I make it out to the driveway as he's opening his truck door. I'm completely out of breath, and it feels like a bus is sitting across my chest as I heave in a huge gulp of air and shout his name.

"Em, what are you doing?" he says, running over to me.

I'm hunched over trying to catch my breath as he pulls me down to sit in his lap, right here in the driveway. He begins rubbing my back, telling me to try and breathe deep and slow. "I didn't … want … you to … leave," I manage to get out.

"I'm sorry, I shouldn't have left so abruptly. You look like you're about to pass out and it's all my fault."

"Lucas ... it's not ... I wanted ..."

My mind won't clear and I'm doing a fucking terrible job of trying to talk to him, so I do the next best thing I can think of. I kiss him. It's not fast or deep because I really would pass out. Instead, it's soft and broken. I need to keep pulling away to take little breaths before pressing my lips back to his. It's probably the worst kiss in the history of kisses, but it's likely the most meaningful one because I'm pretty sure I'm risking suffocation doing it. My mouth hasn't spoken the words I love you, but I think that maybe this kiss just did.

Chapter 17

October 29th, 2013

Dear Diary,

I'm not going to make it to graduation. I thought at the beginning of the year that maybe I could; that if I kept myself well, ate when I was supposed to, drank when I was supposed to, took my meds, I'd have a chance.

Now I think I'd need a miracle.

I once heard someone say that life begins at the end of your comfort zone, but that saying doesn't take into account people like me. I'm completely out of my comfort zone. But there's no guarantee of anything beyond this. Life is now, right this second that I'm sitting here breathing, my lungs inflating and my heart beating.

This is my life.

People shouldn't constantly strive to do things that scare them in a bid to live; their lives will be filled with fear. But they also shouldn't sit around waiting for something epic that sparks their realization that their life has just begun. Life is what happens while you're waiting for it to happen. It's not always extraordinary. Most people won't get to realize all of their hopes and dreams, but they'll be living out new ones they never knew they wanted.

I'm staring at the envelopes, holding the letters that I've written for my parents and Blair. My unfinished bucket list is enclosed in Blair's with a note asking her to complete it. It's been sealed and sitting on my dresser for a week now, but as soon as I have the energy, I need to re-do it. I'm just waiting for a moment when I'm feeling up to it. There's a box on that list that deserves a check, and an explanation of why. Lucas Wade should feature in my letter; he's taught me so much in such a short space of time.

Somewhere in between the silly texts, the random shopping dates, the talking and the laughter, I think I fell in love. I shouldn't be surprised; he promised me that he'd make me fall, and so I waited. I was anticipating an epic moment of realization where I felt dizzy and excited; butterflies would take flight and my heart would skip a beat when he spoke my name. But that's not love—that's lust. And when I think of the way he makes me smile, and the comfort I get from knowing that he's near…that's what love is, or at least it's how I know it to be.

I can't wait to tell him I've finally figured it out.

Lucas

IT'S NOT A good sign to be sitting and talking to yourself in the middle of a field. I'm not crazy; I know this. But it's where I feel most close to you.

You died tonight.

You hadn't returned any of my calls, so I drove to your house. When I pulled up, your Dad came to the door. It was the first time we'd met but he knew who I was. I'm holding onto the thought that you've been talking me up to your parents. He told me that it wasn't a good time; you were inside with your nurses and I should maybe prepare myself to go tell you goodbye.

That one sentence is the worst I've ever heard.

It far outweighs the day the doctors told me my tumor was inoperable. I can deal with shit happening to me; I'm used to it. But to you … it's not right. I wish to fuck I could have changed things for you.

I don't cry. I think the last time I did I was maybe seven. Some punk kid stole my lunch money, and back then it was like the worst thing anyone could ever do to me. This is the part where I need to fess up and tell you that I was a really fat kid up until high school. I loved food. It wasn't the money that made me cry, though, it was that I was with this really skinny kid who looked like maybe his parents didn't have much to begin with. His pants were too short and looked like they were from a thrift store. When the asshole took his cash, too, I got in my first ever fistfight. If you're wondering ... I lost.

When I got home that night and Mom saw my fat lip, she made me tell her what happened. I'll never forget what she said to me when she tucked me into bed that night. She said I was always going to be a lover and not a fighter, and I cried. Not because she'd basically called me a pansy, but because I couldn't stop that asshole from stealing the kid's money. She said to me that I shouldn't waste my tears on hateful people, or situations that were out of my control. From then on, I haven't. But as much as I love you, Emily, I can't stop myself from crying right now.

Shit, I have no idea why I'm saying this. I guess I just want more time. I want to tell you my stories about growing up, but more than that, I want to hear yours. I want to know which lucky guy got your first kiss. Where your favorite place in the whole word is, and what your happiest memories of your childhood are. I hate that you can't tell me. I feel so goddamn helpless. I couldn't fight your cancer for you, and these tears ... fuck, how can they be wasted if I'm spilling them for you? I kissed you while you were sleeping; I sat with you and held your hand. Your mom told me that she was pretty sure you knew what was going on; you were just too exhausted to open your eyes. I need to believe that when I told you I loved you, and you squeezed my hand, that was you saying it back. Wait for me, Emily. Wherever you are, I'll come and find you.

I won't be long.

Blair

"I CAN'T BELIEVE it's been a year that you've been gone. I swear I can still hear your voice when I visit your parents' house. They're doing great, you know. You'd be so proud.

"I guess I should catch you up on some of the gossip. Casey's doing pre-law at Brown. Can you believe that? I don't think anyone took her seriously when she claimed that she was going to be a lawyer after watching *Legally Blonde*!

"Brie is … well, Brie is Brie. Her and Jackson—yeah, you heard me right, have been dating for the past six months and it's going really well. I always claimed that the day Brie got herself a serious boyfriend was the day I'd sign up to do the New York City Marathon naked. Well, I'm not going to streak through Manhattan, but I have signed up. I'm running for Cancer Research, and I've already announced it on Facebook, so I have to go through with it now. Joy.

"I finally read your diary and journals. That sounds wrong, doesn't it? They took me a long time. It was difficult for me to read, knowing they were your words, your hopes and fears. You amaze me, Miss Wilson. I have to admit, I'm sad that we didn't get to talk about Lucas more. I had no idea any of that was going on. I get that you wanted something just for you, but I'd have liked to have spent some time with the boy that stole your heart. He must have been pretty special. I saw him briefly at your funeral, but only in passing. He looked devastated—everyone did. You'll never know how much we all miss you every single day."

"Are you ready, Princess?" Ethan calls from the tree he's propped against; he's giving me time to talk with my Emily alone. I love that he respects our privacy. There are things in a girl's life that can only be shared with her best friend.

"Two minutes, baby," I signal before turning back to Em's plot. I lay the sunflowers I've brought her next to a huge bunch of brightly colored daisies. I pick up the card, and look to see who they're from because they're gorgeous. There's no name and the note simply says, 'Hey, beautiful.'

"I think these are from your boy," I say to Em with a smile. "I have to go, I need to drop Ethan off at a gig, but I'll be back soon, Emily … I promise."

Throughout the Promises series, you meet Emily, Blair and Ethan. Although their stories are fictitious, the problems that they have to overcome are very real. If you have been affected by any of the issues raised in this or any of my books, there is always someone here to listen and help.

CANCER SUPPORT:

Macmillan Cancer Support –
http://www.macmillan.org.uk/Home.aspx

Leukemia and Lymphoma Society –
http://www.lls.org

DOMESTIC VIOLENCE AND ABUSE SUPPORT:

Childhelp National Child Abuse Hotline –
https://www.childhelp.org/hotline/

The National Domestic Violence Hotline –
http://www.thehotline.org

Thank YOU

IT IS KIND of a tradition now, that I start my acknowledgements with an apology to my amazing husband and children: I'm sorry—again. I broke my promises—again. You know by now that if my laptop is open, you need to fend for yourselves. Believe me when I tell you that I know how lucky I am, you're all so understanding and patient. I love you, guys. You are my world.

Author Kathryn Andrews, my book bestie... Fist bump! Book #3 can you even believe it? I don't need to tell you how awesome you are, you should already know. xoxo

To all the wonderful bloggers that have loved the Promises series, your support astounds me, you rock!

The Perusing Princesses, Elizabeth, Kelly and Emma; If you count all the waves, in all the oceans, that's how much I love you gals.

My BETA team! Dana, Susan, Ali, Trish, Jen and Megan. WOW, just wow. I never in a million years, expected the reactions to this book that I received. I'm blessed to have you all in my corner.

To my best friend and sister-in-law, Lucy. You know

I'm officially Mrs. Last Minute, but you always drop what you're doing to help me out anyway. Love you!

The Pimpers… Author Anne Mercier, Dana, Sanne, Alexis, Susan, Heather, Pauline, Lynn, Irma and Ali. Thank you for telling everyone about my books. You girls never fail to make me smile. I can't express in words, how grateful I am. (which is kind of ironic, considering words are my thing!)

The wonderfully talented *Melissa Gill* of MGBOOK-COVERS & DESIGNS. You knocked it out of the park AGAIN!

Jennifer Roberts-Hall Thank you for your wonderful editing skills, you are like super woman! You climb mountains and then go home and edit. I'd climb a mountain and then go home and die!

Marie Piquette You are a dream to work with. I know I can always depend on you, and I can't commend you highly enough!

Julie (JT Formatting) my brilliant formatter, you are the most helpful person in the world—EVER.

Finally, a huge thank you, to you the reader. It's truly astounding to me, that you're reading my third book, after loving the others. I am so humbled.

FOR INFORMATION ABOUT ELLE BROOKS
AND HER BOOKS, VISIT:

Her Website: http://ellebrooksauthor.com
Twitter: https://twitter.com/@ellebrooksautho
E-mail: ellebrooksauthor@gmail.com
Facebook: https://facebook.com/elle.brooks.author
Goodreads: https://Goodreads.com/Elle_Brooks

THE PROMISES SERIES:

Book #1 *Promises Hurt*
Book #2 *Forgotten Promises*
Book #3 *Empty Promises*

Reveal – A New Adult contemporary romance,
coming mid-2015.